ABOUT
STEVEN J YEO

Steven J Yeo is a published playwright with pantomimes and plays being performed all over the world. Keterlyn is his debut novel.

Dedicated to my father,
who never got to read this book.
Thanks to Tony Small, the best teacher of all.

To sheila,

lovely to meet you!

FORESHORE
Classic Short Fiction

STEVEN J YEO

KETERLYN

FORESHORE PUBLISHING
London

Published by Foreshore Publishing 2022.
The home of quality short fiction.

Foreshore Publishing

The Forge 397-411 Westferry Road,
Isle of Dogs, London, E14 3AE

Foreshore Publishing Limited Reg. No. 13358650

ISBN 978-1-7395930-5-6

Edited by Simon Ives.

WWW.FORESHOREPUBLISHING.COM

1

GRAHAM SMITH WOUND HIS way down a single dirt track running through a ten-acre field of knee-high grass. A strongly built farmer in his fifties with salt and peppered hair, he wore jeans and a black t-shirt bearing the legend "Fifty with Shades of Grey" in bold white letters.

This early morning walk with his dog allowed him to check the farm's fencing and enjoy the autumn sunshine.

"Jasper." He paused and, when there was no sign of the dog, tried again. "Here boy." Graham increased his pace to catch up with him. "I'm getting bored with this game," he muttered.

Just then he was alerted by Jasper's barking. He crossed the boundary grass, jogging towards a wooded area. As he reached an incline overlooking the trees he came to a halt. The barking had stopped and the few seconds that passed as he scanned the treeline seemed like an eternity.

Suddenly Jasper appeared, yelping as he came bounding up the incline. The dog rushed through Graham's legs, unbalancing him and sending him rolling down the slope, before coming to rest on leafy ground just inside the trees.

"Jesus Jasper! What's up with you?" Getting to his feet and dusting himself off, Graham looked around him. His mouth fell open in horror at the sight before him.

***

1284 LOWER SAXONY GERMANY

The morning mist lingered through the trees clinging to the leafy carpet like wisps of spent smoke, slowly dissipating into the surrounding autumnal colours. The sun, forcing its way through the canopy of leaves, shone patchily onto the ancient oaks and maples, streaking through the mist. A bird screeched into flight as the sound of short, sharp, crunching pierced the stillness and a pair of tiny bare feet ran past.

A wide-eyed young girl, no more than six or seven, puffed and panted through gritted teeth as she darted between the tall trees. Her long blond hair, dirty and matted, flowed behind her as she cracked twigs and branches beneath her unflinching feet.

Her dirty and ragged knee-length dress snagged on a low-lying branch, causing her to pause for a moment to free it. As she tugged it loose, she looked behind her before dashing off in a different direction. Her dirty face, streaked by tear tracks, glistened as she cast quick glances to either side.

She came to a sudden halt when a huge deer appeared on the path, directly in front of her. She raised a finger to her lips, willing the creature to silence, before scampering past. The distant barking and yelping of dogs began to fill the woods.

The girl came to her destination, a rocky outcrop shielded by trees and well hidden by dense foliage. She made for a small opening at the base of the outcrop, a narrow passageway that she could just manage to crawl into on her hands and knees.

Crawling into the black interior she soon found she could manage a crouched walk before finally being able to run forward down a damp tunnel which eventually opened into a small cave, illuminated by phosphorescent veins in the rock walls.

The cavern had a few home comforts scattered about. A log could easily pass for a table and had a small wooden cup and some mouldy crusts of bread resting on it. To one side was an area of dry leaves and grass which could easily pass for a giant bird's nest.

Outside the cave the dogs barking grew louder and voices could be heard. Four burly men gathered there, together with three terriers, restrained by sturdy chains. "Release the hounds," came the shout, and the three small dogs excitedly bolted into the cave's mouth, eager to reach the source of the scent they followed.

Meanwhile the little girl desperately searched the leafy bedding. What she found was a small blue stone, worn down and unnatural, a peculiar deep shade of sky blue. She clutched it tightly to her chest and it began to glow, softly pulsating.

The dogs rushed into the cavern, slipping on the hard floor. Confused, they sniffed relentlessly around the walls and buried their noses in the rough bedding. The trail came to an abrupt end in this empty cave.

Outside, one of the men recalled the dogs from their fruitless task and the hounds, barking furiously, raced back through the dank tunnel and into the sunlight.

The little girl re-appeared, out of sight of her friends playing on the edge of a small hamlet of houses at the other side of the huge forest. She ran into the middle of the laughing children as they played as a group. Several children called out her name as she joined them. "Keterlyn" they called to her. Greeting her with outstretched hands and smiles.

One child had her eyes covered and was trying to touch any other child to make it their turn to be blindfolded, while the others poked and prodded her trying not to be caught. Play continued until the sound of wonderful music could be heard in the distance, getting louder and sweeter to their ears. It was so sweet and wonderful the children started to dance, laughing and smiling as they did so. Keterlyn also found herself bewitched by the music and started dancing with her friends.

Soon the dancing formed a long line as children started appearing from all directions. Dozens and dozens of them danced into the line and one by one they danced away into the forest, until the last child had made their way into the forest and was gone.

***

A black and tan Jack Russell ran out of the woods and away into the long grass. Graham emerged looking peaky, scurrying as fast as he could away from the trees.

"Wait for me boy," he called, on the verge of tears. "Wait for me."

He ran as fast as he could through the field, chasing Jasper's distant barking. He soon reached the five-bar gate with wire fencing either side and threw himself over it. Before him was a large stone-built farmhouse from the turn of the 20th century.

There were two large silos to the left, slightly behind, and a large metal barn to the right, partially obscured by the Massey Ferguson tractor parked in front of it. From the gate a dirt track led to three stone steps onto a wooden porch.

Graham ran along the track, leapt up the steps and rushed into the house, closing the door behind him. Somewhere in the distance Jasper continued barking.

2

THE AUTUMN SHOWERS HAD blessed the lush banks of rolling grass outside the University with a deep green, fresh look. The flower beds were well-fed and nurtured, the blooms colourfully spelling out 'UWE'.

Dr Tony Small was a fit and healthy-looking man in his early fifties. Some may have thought him younger but his slightly greying hair, varifocal glasses and the checked jacket, complete with leather patches at the elbows, gave away his true generation.

Inside the lecture hall Dr Small had covered two large whiteboards with scribblings about Adolf Hitler, Heinrich Himmler and various pseudo religious relics. Twenty or thirty fresh faced students sat unfazed by the illegibility of the words. They were more concerned with the pearls of wisdom their tutor was passing on to them.

"Hitler and Himmler were obsessed with the Ghent altarpiece, believing it to be a map to the so-called Arma Christi, the instruments of Christ's passion. Among these relics were the Holy Grail, the Crown of Thorns and the Spear of Destiny."

Small drew a thick line under Hitler's name. "Now if Hitler had any of these relics paraded at the front of his army, he believed he would be invincible, as he could call on religious backing."

In large letters on the whiteboard, he wrote the words "The Ahnenerbe."

"This gave rise to Himmler's Ahnenerbe, which roughly translates as the inheritance of the forefathers or the ancestral inheritance."

A bell sounded as he finished speaking. Some of the students began noisily standing, forcing Dr Small to raise his voice.

"Research the Ahnenerbe for next time and write five hundred words on why it was doomed to fail. The essay will count towards your Finals."

There were a few grunts and a scramble of feet as the students made their exit. Dr Small began erasing everything he had written on the whiteboards, a simple house rule that not everybody seemed capable of following. Another of life's small frustrations, he thought.

A blonde-haired student, thin and wiry, stood patiently waiting for the tutor to acknowledge him.

"Ah, Russell."

"Sir, I read your last book …"

"So you were the one?" said Small with a smile.

"Yes sir," Russell replied, missing the joke entirely. "You come across in the book as a disbeliever in the paranormal and I wondered why that was? Especially given that your job is a lecturer in Paranormal Studies."

"Good question Russell," Small replied, taking a moment to consider a fuller response. "Take this pen," he said, holding up a whiteboard marker. "To you or me it is simply that, a pen."

"Yes sir."

"But what if I told you it was a weapon that could kill you in less than two minutes? You'd have a hard time believing that wouldn't you?"

"Yes sir," replied Russell, clearly puzzled.

"But if, hypothetically of course, I were to drive it into someone's neck, severing their main artery, and we were to watch them bleed out in just a few short seconds, then you would believe it was a weapon."

"Sir?"

"Look, it's the same for me with the paranormal. Show me a ghost or somebody who can move solid objects with their mind, so I can feel it, see it and sense it for myself, and I'll believe it. Until then it's just someone telling a story."

Russell continued to look puzzled.

"All paranormal activity is, one," holding up his thumb, "explained away as trickery or fake by science or, two," forming a finger gun with his pointing finger, "cannot be proved to be real as there is no evidence or comparisons yet available."

Small fired the imaginary gun before holding it to his lips and blowing his fingertip.

"Now off you go and impress me with your knowledge of the Ahnenerbe."

"Thank you, sir. I'll try," said Russell, holding the door open for his mentor.

"Remember Russell, do or don't but never try."

"Yes, I'll try sir," said Russell as he joined the flood of students heading towards the canteen.

Dr Small shook his head and turned to walk against the tide, a small smile playing on his lips.

He soon reached a single paned glass door bearing the words Dr T Small B.Sc. (Hons), M.Sc., Ph.D., C. Psychologist in gold lettering. Small entered, closing the door behind him.

A short time later there was a rap at the door.

"If you can't walk through it, open it," said Small.

The door opened and Small found himself looking at the UWE Chancellor, Professor Stephen Williams. He was in his sixties, clearly overweight, with thinning hair wearing rimless glasses and a smart dark blue suit with one of the university ties.

"Still pretending to work here Tony?"

"Stephen, when did you get back?" asked Small, rising from his desk to shake the hand the Professor offered.

"About an hour ago."

"And of course, you just had to come here before heading home."

"Of course. How have you been Tony?"

"Busy, believe it or not. Catching up on all these unmarked papers that should have been dealt with weeks ago. But don't tell the Chancellor," Small added with a conspiratorial wink. Gesturing for the Professor to take a seat Small sat back down. "How did it go? Did you get the all clear?"

Williams lost his smile and turned his attention to the book-lined shelves behind his friend's desk. "Not exactly," he said. "But how did the book launch go? Another best seller?"

Small left his desk to stand behind the older man, resting his hand on his shoulder and giving it a gentle squeeze.

"A great launch and a few good book signings but it's too early to tell. We'll know by Tuesday." He moved to the door, making sure it was fully closed.

"Before I forget," said Williams, "a call came in while you were in the hall. I said I'd bring it along as I was coming this way," he added, passing over a note. "It didn't make any sense to me, so I expect you'll have to call them back."

Small studied the note, then tucked it into his breast pocket before taking his seat behind his desk. "What does 'not exactly' mean Stephen?"

The Professor stood, moved to the door and opened it. "Same crap, different day, that's all. Now don't work too hard and don't forget to call them back," he said, indicating his friend's jacket pocket. "It sounds urgent. We can catch up later."

Williams left the room, closing the door behind him. Small sat with a worried look on his face as he watched him leave.

3

TONY SMALL ARRIVED IN his dark blue BMW 525, parked it and began on foot towards the farmhouse. He passed several police cars, ambulances and coroner's vans that littered the farm road. As he walked along the dirt track, he stopped a passing PC.

"DI Janet Walsh?"

The PC pointed towards a field. The five-bar gate stood open and a visible vehicle trail led across the field to a wooded area. Dozens of uniformed police officers dressed in bright yellow hazmat suits trailed to and from the woods like so many ants. Tony set off purposefully along the track, carefully avoiding the officers as he went.

At the entrance to the trees a wide area of tall grass had been flattened by the constant pedestrian traffic. An eighteen wheeled articulated vehicle straddled the flattened area, "Police Mobile Command Unit" emblazoned along its side.

A PC raised a hand and stopped Tony.

"This area is off limits to the public sir."

Tony chose his words carefully so as not to say the wrong thing. He had history with the police from his youth which he preferred not to recall. It had left him with a slight distrust.

"I was asked to come here by DI Janet Walsh as a matter of urgency. My name is Dr Tony Small."

"Ah yes sir, go on down," said the officer pointing the way. "She's just inside the treeline and she's expecting you. You can't miss her."

Tony made his way around the command unit and headed for the trees, trying to avoid bumping into the police in hazmat suits. At the edge of the flattened grass he stopped for a moment to compose himself before setting off into the woods.

His line of work had taken him to many strange locations, haunted houses and religious rituals, exhumations and exorcisms. This was the first time he had been called to a farmhouse surrounded by what seemed to be the entire local police force, though, and his interest was well and truly piqued.

Glancing to his right Tony saw a young officer throwing up into weeds at the bottom of a tree. Nearby another was sat with his head in his hands being comforted by a colleague.

Puzzled, Tony took what seemed a leap of faith and strode down the grass incline into the trees. He was greeted by a truly horrible and morbid sight. Generator controlled lights illuminated dozens of children's bodies hanging from the trees, in various stages of undress.

Some hung by the neck, others by bound hands and feet. Many of them looked as though they had been hanging for quite some time. Flesh hung from their sides and faces as if it had been ripped from them by animals and wildlife. Yet others looked fresh as if they had been put up just a few hours ago.

Ages varied from two or three to twelve or thirteen. There were simply too many bodies for Tony to count.

A touch on his arm made him jump.

He was confronted by a beautiful auburn-haired woman, apparently in her forties, dressed in a hazmat suit without a hood.

"Doctor Small I presume. I'm Janet Walsh. I called you."

"Oh yes, hello," he said, offering his hand.

"Not a pretty sight is it?" She appeared to be studying his face, looking for a reaction.

"Should I be wearing one of those?" he asked, pointing to her yellow suit.

"It isn't needed, to be honest. This isn't a crime scene." She gestured at the bodies. "Take a closer look."

Tony walked around the trees, studying the bodies one by one. Several minutes passed before he noticed one of the police officers pass his hand through a young boy's body as if it were a hologram.

A young girl of five or six hung by her neck directly in front of Tony. He slowly reached out to touch her and saw his hand pass straight through before connecting with the bark of the tree.

He moved to another body, an older boy hanging much higher up in a tree. He reached for his blood-stained feet but once more felt only rough bark.

"What the hell is this?" he said, looking to the DI for inspiration.

"We were hoping you could tell us Doctor Small."

"I don't understand what is happening here." Once more he reached out to a body using both hands this time. He found only the tree and his own hand.

"These were all found here yesterday by the farmer walking his dog. Seventy-three girls and fifty-seven boys, one hundred and thirty in total. Ages range from three to thirteen or so. We can't touch them or smell them. Hell, we can't even cut them down. We can only look and leave them like this.

"That's why we called the University, looking for someone who's used to dealing with this kind of weird stuff. Any ideas doc?"

Tony moved from child to child, studying them. A small girl hung lower than those on either side of her, her head level with his. She was maybe six, dirty blond hair wearing a torn, ankle length white dress with bare legs and feet. Looking closely at her face he could make out dried tear tracks.

She blinked.

"Jesus, she blinked. Did you see that?"

"I thought I saw something similar about an hour ago, doctor. Under these circumstances it's easy to see things that aren't there."

"No, she actually blinked. Honestly!" Waving his arms through her he touched only tree.

DI Walsh moved closer until all three faces were mere inches apart. The girl opened her eyes and gulped in a mouthful of air. The DI stumbled backwards and fell as Tony clutched his chest as if he had been shot.

"Jesus Christ! I think I've peed myself," she said, gingerly getting to her feet.

"You and me both," replied Tony. "Is she alive?" He reached out again but this time his hand felt flesh. He seized her legs, lifting to take the pressure off the rope round her neck.

"She's real! My god she's real. Cut her down!"

DI Walsh fumbled with the rope while the girl, seemingly scared, struggled frantically.

"Medic! We need help here," she screamed.

Medical help soon arrived and the rope was untied. Tony grabbed the girl who continued to struggle before exhaustedly lapsing into unconsciousness in his cradling arms.

"Hang on in there little one," said Tony, passing the unconscious body to the medic.

Having laid her on a nearby gurney the medic checked for a pulse.

"She's alive," he called. "Very dehydrated but she should be okay. Physically anyway."

"How is this possible doctor?"

"I don't know," Tony replied.

"Never mind. Get her to Gloucester Royal as fast as you can and keep someone with her at all times." Turning to Tony she said, "What just happened?"

"You peed your pants is what."

"Look, I'm still shaking," she said, holding out her hands.

"Let's hope she'll be okay. She looked a feisty little thing."

Tony paused, looking back at the other children hanging limply from the trees.

"You know I've spent my career uncovering the truth behind so-called paranormal activities. The lies and fraud I've come across. In my experience ninety per cent of all such activity is created by people or nature. But I've never heard or seen anything that comes close to what I've witnessed today."

"And the other ten per cent?"

Tony moved towards the remaining children. "Unexplained because we just don't know enough or have the scientific answers. Do you think there are any more alive or was she the only one?"

Tony frantically rushed amongst the bodies, running his hands through their insubstantial forms one by one. Tears started to stream down his face as he pushed a policeman aside. Realising what was happening, the DI intervened.

"Dr Small." He ignored her. "Dr Small," she called again. Finally, "Tony!"

He came to a halt at the body of a badly mutilated four-year-old. Her chest was open and skin had been peeled from her tiny face so that it touched her shoulders. Overcome at last, he dropped to his knees, openly weeping.

"Come on Tony. We need to walk away for a minute. It's a lot for anyone to take in." Helping him to his feet she added, "Let's compose ourselves and come back in a while."

Taking his arm she led him to the Mobile Command Unit. They both sat on the steps while he wiped the tears away.

"What happened here?" he asked. "How is this happening? How was the girl not here one minute then suddenly here the next? And what happened to that other poor little one?"

"You're supposed to be the expert here, Tony. Sort yourself out and then help us understand it."

Tony took a couple of deep breaths and a large sniff before smiling at the DI.

"I'm sorry. It was the state of that poor baby back there."

"I understand. I was the same this morning. It's awful."

"Right, I can't do this on my own. I'm going to need help on this one."

"We'll get you all the help you need Doctor, just name it."

"No, I want my own team on this one. They'll need to take readings and photos and run a few tests. Lots of tests." He smiled at the DI. "It's the only way. We have to study, analyse and document it all."

She stood. "As long as they can be trusted. We're going to need to keep this under wraps for the time being, at least until we can understand what has happened or is still happening here."

Tony nodded and held out his hand. The DI helped him to his feet. Taking his phone from his pocket, he tapped the screen. When it began ringing, he turned on the speaker so they could both hear the conversation.

"Johnathan and his team will be most helpful, I'm sure of it. I was very grateful for their assistance the last time we worked together."

The quiet air of professionalism was shattered as soon as the phone was answered.

"Yo! Ghostbusters!"

"I thought we agreed you can't call yourselves that Johnathan," said Tony, slightly embarrassed.

"Yo, Doctor Small. Is the book out yet? I hope you gave us a good write up."

"Of course! You should receive a few copies from the publishers in a couple of days."

"That's amazing, perfect timing. We're almost out of toilet paper."

Tony groaned.

"Only kidding. What's up Doc?"

"Listen, I've got a good one for you here. You'll need all the gear and I do mean all of it. Who's there at the moment?"

"I've got Jim Bob, Matt and Sally. Why?"

"Okay. Bring the guys but leave Sally to man the office."

"Alright, man, but she won't like it."

"Just bring everything you've got and leave Sally there. For now at least."

The DI gave Tony a puzzled look.

"I'll explain everything when you get here and I'll text the address over. And hurry!"

"Why not Sally?" asked the DI.

"Her four year old died in a road accident a few months back. Died in her arms, covered in blood by the side of the road. She isn't up to seeing all this."

"Who is? We both need a break. Fancy a coffee while we wait?"

Tony sent his text.

"Coffee?" she repeated.

"Sorry, coffee. Yes please. Lead the way."

4

THE LITTLE GIRL'S screams reverberated around Room 226 and into the rest of the Psychiatric Ward of Gloucester Royal Hospital. She had been connected to a heart monitor and had a saline drip in her arm. Clearly scared, she had removed the monitor pads as well as the drip.

Two nurses rushed in to either side of the bed.

"It's okay, baby. We've got you now," said one in a softly spoken voice. "You're safe now. No-one is going to hurt you."

In response the girl babbled long sentences of a foreign language.

"Is that German?" said the second nurse.

"We don't understand you sweetie. Do you speak English?" The first nurse gently stroked the girl's arm.

The girl merely continued her tirade. One word seemed to stand out as it was repeated so often: Rattenfanger.

"If she doesn't calm down, we'll have to sedate her."

Frantically the little girl struggled to free herself from the firm grip of the nurses, startling at every beep and flickering light of the machines around her.

"Okay we need to sedate her," said the first nurse. "She'll cause herself harm if she carries on. Go on, I've got her." She grasped both of the girl's arms as her colleague administered the sedative.

The girl became noticeably calmer as the minutes ticked by. Muttering "Rattenfanger, Rattenfanger," she finally quietened and slumped onto her pillow, to soon fall asleep.

The nurses efficiently rearranged the bedclothes and replaced the pads and drip. Smoothing the girl's hair, the second nurse asked again, "Was that German she was speaking?"

"I don't know," replied the first. "Poor kid was terrified of this lot though," she added, pointing at the machinery in the room. "I'd guess she's never been in hospital before."

"Well she can't stay sedated forever. We'll have to let the doctor know." The second nurse held up a bright blue stone. "What are we going to do with this? I found it in the pocket of her dress when we were putting her to bed."

"It probably means something to her. Leave it on the table there so she can see it when she wakes up."

The blue stone was placed on the bedside table in clear sight of the girl. As the nurses withdrew to continue their duties around the ward, it began to gently glow.

5

A WAILING SIREN COULD be heard approaching. Suddenly a jet-black hearse came into view, siren horns on the roof, scattering stones and dust as it sped down the dirt track. It didn't slow down as it entered the field and alert police had to swiftly get out of its way. Finally it side skidded to a halt in front of the Command Unit, the sirens falling silent.

As the plume of dust and dirt settled around the hearse, a distorted Ghostbusters logo on the bonnet reading "Ghostdusters" became visible. The driver's door opened and Johnathon stepped out, removing his blue-tinted Lennon sunglasses as he did so. He was in his thirties, plump with blond unkempt hair and stubble, dressed in a green boiler suit with matching wellington boots.

"Now that's how to make an entrance," said DI Walsh.

"Maybe I should have mentioned he's a bit eccentric," said Tony.

"No, I love it," she said, smiling.

Tony appeared confused by her response and watched as she approached Johnathon, holding out her hand in greeting. He promptly took it, turned it over and kissed her palm.

"My lady, take me to your leader. Or to your bed," he said.

With Johnathon still holding her hand, she turned to Tony open-mouthed.

"This is Detective Inspector Janet Walsh, Johnathon. She is the most senior officer here today." Tony paused for effect. "And is our boss."

"Not only are you the most senior here, my lady, but you are also by far the loveliest."

"Now, I do like him," she said to Tony.

Johnathon kissed her hand once more before returning it to her. The rest of the team had quietly assembled behind him. He introduced them with a wave.

"This is Matt who runs all our instruments." He pointed out a slim Asian in his early twenties wearing thick-lensed glasses and an identical boiler suit and wellingtons.

"It's Matté, actually," he said, holding out his hand. "My parents were French and Japanese, but Johnathon won't let me have the accent until I've served three years with him.

The DI smiled at the absurdity of it whilst shaking his hand.

"Three years, Matt. I told you." Johnathon indicated the third member of the team. "And this is our gofer, Jim Bob, or Ginger Beard as we like to call him. After the infamous pirate, Captain Ginger Beard."

Jim Bob sported the company issue green boiler suit and wellingtons. He clearly got his nickname from his long ginger hair and matching bushy beard, belying his young years.

"How many more times, it's Blackbeard the pirate."

"Nope, it's definitely Ginger Beard. You can't prove otherwise."

"Actually," Matté interjected, "the history books confirm that Blackbeard was actually a real figure, Edward Teach."

A lengthy debate ensued as the three argued their individual cases and the merits of piratical authenticity, until Tony interjected.

"Lads, can we just agree he was a pirate and leave it at that. We've got work to do."

"Lead us to it, boss," said Johnathon, grabbing a meter from the hearse, while the other two each picked up a flight case.

Tony led them to the wooded area before coming to a sudden stop, causing Johnathon to bump into him.

"Could you at least try to look professional, Johnathon."

"Sorry Doc. I was concentrating on taking readings."

As the others caught up Tony spoke. "Now guys, this is why I didn't want Sally here."

"Boy, is she upset with you Doc," said Jim Bob.

"She'll thank me later," said Tony, knowing the team was about to encounter something none of them had ever experienced before. "Inside this wood are the bodies of one hundred and thirty children, hanging from the trees."

Nobody spoke.

"Did you hear what I said?"

"One hundred and thirty dead kids tied to trees," said Johnathon, studying his meter. "Got it."

"Oh whatever," said Tony, waving his arms to usher them towards the woods.

The three Ghostdusters entered first, stepping down the slight incline leading to the trees. None of the three seemed upset or worried by the situation. If anything they appeared to be excited by the peculiar circumstances they found themselves in.

"It's some kind of echo manifesting itself on the here and now," suggested Matté.

"No, it's obviously a sophisticated holographic projection," said Jim Bob. "Look," he added, running his hand through one of the bodies.

"The clarity of the images is amazing. This is some piece of kit!" said Johnathon. "Do we get to keep it? You know, finders keepers?"

"Bagsy the projection unit," said Matté.

"I'll have the hard drive," Johnathon said.

"So I'll get whatever's left I suppose," added Jim Bob.

The three of them were constantly on the move, looking up trees, behind bushes, anywhere that might hold the source of the images. Tony and DI Walsh left them to it.

"Kids, eh?" said Tony. "I think we'd best leave them to it for now. They'll get there. Coffee?"

"Yes, why not? It's your turn to buy."

"Oh. I thought it was free."

Looking back the DI added "But shouldn't you, er …"

"No, not yet. Give them a couple of hours to set up their gear and take some readings. We'll join them again when they've calmed down a bit and started scratching their heads.

6

FRANKE SCHWARTZ-FREUD HAD been a child psychologist at the Gloucester Royal for almost ten years now. She had seen kids come and go, helping most if not all. She had a slim, athletic build, great skin, long dark brown hair and hazel eyes. Today she wore a two-piece charcoal grey suit over a white blouse.

She was good at her job and usually first choice when it came to the difficult cases, like this one. Having studied body language under Alan Pease she found it easy to put children at their ease, avoiding complicated conversations and language problems.

Franke was seated at the bedside of the little girl who was no longer surrounded by machines and tech. She slept. A nurse sat attentively at the foot of the bed.

The bed had been moved to the corner against a wall and the room seemed bigger because of it. The bright blue stone sat on the bedside table at the head of the bed.

The girl began to wake and Franke motioned for the nurse to leave them alone. She had been told that the girl seemed to speak German so Franke, whose second language that was, tried some simple phrases.

"It's okay," she said softly. "You are safe now. Safe."

The little girl was clearly frightened and sat up quickly, squeezing herself into the corner. Her eyes scanned the room as if seeking out an escape route.

"You are safe," Franke continued in German, touching her chest as she did so. "Franke. Friend." The girl appeared to relax a little so she repeated the phrase. "Franke, friend."

The girl tilted her head slightly, as if trying to understand. She ran her hands over the sheets and pillows then, spotting the blue stone, startled Franke by reaching across the bed to grab it. Clasping it tight in one hand, she touched her chest with the other. "Keterlyn," she said. "Keterlyn."

The girl pointed at her. "Franke," she said, then pointed at her own chest. "Keterlyn."

Franke realised she was making progress. "Franke," she said again, pointing at herself and "Keterlyn," pointing at the girl. She smiled and was rewarded with a beautiful grin from the girl, encouraging Franke to press on.

"Where are you from? Where are your parents? Mummy and Daddy?"

Keterlyn repeated the words "Mummy. Daddy," then began speaking at a frantic rate that Franke didn't have a hope of following.

Franke's grasp of German was good and she could understand most regional dialects. What Keterlyn was speaking was very unusual, although some German words could be made out.

"Slow down, I can't understand you," said Franke but the girl ignored her and continued her incomprehensible monologue. After a minute or two she stopped. Franke shrugged her shoulders, using her body language to indicate that she couldn't understand her.

"I am sorry but I can't understand you," Franke said. "I think you are speaking German but I can't understand it and I don't know why." She frowned to indicate to the girl that she was sad.

Keterlyn held out her hand.

"You want me to hold your hand?" asked Franke. "I'm not really supposed to."

Keterlyn waggled her hand at Franke who eventually took it in hers. As the girl held her hand in a vice-like grip, she moved the one holding the blue stone to her chest. Franke looked on in amazement as the stone turned yellow, shining brightly.

Then a voice began to whisper. The girl's lips weren't moving. Franke looked around her but the room was empty save for the two of them. The voice grew louder and clearer.

"My name is Keterlyn. I am very scared. Can you help me?"

Franke dropped the girl's hand and jumped to her feet, knocking her chair over as she did so.

"How are you doing that?"

The girl offered her hand again. Franke reset her chair and sat down. After a moment she took the hand in hers.

"Please don't be frightened. I was confused before. Can you understand me now?"

Franke nodded. "How are you doing this?"

Keterlyn smiled proudly. "I'm a witch," she said.

7

THE GHOSTDUSTERS SAT ON flight cases, huddled around a legless kettle-shaped BBQ which they used as a fire pit, flames leaping from it. Tony and DI Walsh sat on a log opposite. Johnathon was holding a sheaf of papers in his hand.

"We got no readings from the kids or the surrounding landscape," he said. "There's no electronic interference of any sort."

"Yes, and we got really sensitive readings too," added Matté. "We really freaked out when Jim Bob's watch got in the way, that's how sensitive it is."

"Thanks Matt," Johnathon said. "There were no temperature variations, no EMF, no radiation and no humidity anomalies."

"No negative ion readings, no static electricity and no infra sound," said Matté.

"Yep, we got nothing. Except that tree," said Jim Bob.

Tony looked at each of the three in turn, trying not to react.

"The tree?" he said, glancing at the DI.

"What about the tree?" she said, casually returning Tony's look.

Johnathon pointed at Jim Bob and said, "Now captain, how many times have I told you not to divulge sensitive information? That's our job," he added, indicating Matté and himself.

"Sorry boss," said Jim Bob, scratching his ginger beard and standing up. "I know. Go get the ginger beers."

"And don't forget the crackers," said Johnathon.

The DI shook her head in disbelief. "The tree, Johnathon. The tree."

"A watched kettle gathers no more moss than a bird in the hand," he replied with a smile. "Patience is not a sin, my lady." He drew a sheet from the papers he was holding and handed it to Tony. "This is what we got from all the other trees and the children."

"There's nothing here," said Tony, turning it over. "It's blank."

"Exactly. You catch on quick doc. But when we took the readings from the tree with the rope but no kid, this is what we got." Johnathon passed all the rest of the paperwork to Tony.

"All this?"

"Yes, we hit the jackpot on everything. There's something special about that tree. We just haven't found out what yet."

Tony smiled at the DI who nodded. "Well maybe we beat you to it this time," he said. "We know something you don't."

Johnathan leapt to his feet, threw his hands in the air and started pacing up and down.

"For God's sake, doc. How can I work when I don't have all the information? I'm a professional but you're treating me like an amateur. It's just not fair."

Tantrum over, he sat back down, folded his arms and crossed his legs, like a child at a school assembly.

"We had to know if there was anything wrong with the rest of the scene before we told you," said DI Walsh.

"Now you're telling us that there is something special about that tree," added Tony. "We can confidently say that she may be the key to all this."

Johnathon stood again, looking at the pair of them.

"She. You said she. Come on, doc. You've got me dribbling like a horny rabbit."

"Yes doc," added Matté. "You must tell us."

The pair stood, each with their hands clasped together as if praying.

"Please, please, please," they said in unison, then dropped to their knees. "Please, please, please."

"Okay I'll tell you, for God's sake," said Tony. "Now, are you sitting comfortably?"

They scrambled back to sit on the flight cases.

"Then I'll begin."

Johnathon got to his feet again.

"Wait," he said, looking across the field to where Jim Bob stood chatting to a young WPC.

"Oh captain!" shouted Johnathon. "Where's my ginger beer and crackers?"

With an acknowledging wave Jim Bob started to make his way to the hearse, looking back at the girl and making the phone call gesture. Johnathon glared at him before sitting once more.

"Sorry doc," he said. "Carry on."

"Right," said Tony. "When I got here this morning there was a young girl of around six years old hanging from her neck on that tree. Just like the rest of them." He lent forward to gauge the reaction of his avid listeners. "Then suddenly … she opened her eyes and became a real, living child in front of our eyes. I kid you not."

The Ghostdusters appeared mesmerised.

"Then what happened?" asked Matté.

The DI interrupted. "He peed his pants."

Everyone burst out laughing, except Tony who gave the DI a look of disdain.

"So then what? Come on, man, don't leave me in suspense," said Johnathon.

"We lifted her down from the tree, took the rope from around her neck and she was rushed to Gloucester Royal," said Tony.

"So she was real from the start," said Matté.

"No way," said Johnathon. "She couldn't have been a ghost one minute and then real. Impossible."

"When I saw her blink, I passed my hand through her body," said Tony. "She was definitely not real. But when she took a breath, I held her in my arms. I could feel her weight, smell her sweat and hear her screams before she passed out."

"No way, man," said Johnathon.

"It's true," said the DI. "I was there and I saw it too."

Johnathon and Matté knelt before Tony, prostrating themselves. "We are not worthy. We are not worthy," they chanted together.

"I missed a close encounter of the first and second kind," said Johnathon. "You lucky sod."

Matté took Tony's hand and began shaking it vigorously. "You're my hero doc."

Jim Bob chose this moment to arrive, two bottles of ginger beer in each hand, one under his arm and a bag of chips clenched between his teeth. He dropped the chips at Johnathon's feet.

"What did I miss?" he asked, handing out the bottles.

"Well as much fun as this is, I have reports to write," said the DI getting to her feet. "We'll meet in the morning for a catch up."

"And I've got lectures tomorrow that I need to prepare for," said Tony, also standing. "There's a lot of research to be done and plenty of thinking too."

"No lectures for you, doctor," said the DI. "I've spoken to Professor Williams and he's given you three days to assist us."

Tony gave a slight scowl. "Okay then we'll meet here again in the morning. And you three behave yourselves."

The Ghostdusters clinked their bottles in mock salute.

"Come on. I'll walk you to your car," said Tony.

"Who said chivalry is dead?" the DI replied, linking arms. They walked the few steps back to the Command Unit. "Well, this is me," she added.

She stepped into the unit, closing the door behind her, only to reopen it a moment later to confront the startled Tony.

"I live in Tewkesbury and I'm damned if I'm going to drive all that way now," she said. "There's a bunk in here so I'll crash here tonight. You can take me to see the girl in the morning if you'd like."

"Of course, inspector," said Tony, smiling.

"You don't work for me so please call me Janet. Goodnight Tony." She closed the door again.

Tony headed for his car and home.

8

ROOM 226 HAD BEEN transformed into a child's playroom. Toys and board games were scattered around the room but appeared untouched. A large plastic playhouse stood in the corner, seemingly neglected.

Franke and Keterlyn sat deep in conversation, now able to fully understand each other.

"How old are you Keterlyn? When is your birthday?"

Keterlyn was puzzled. "I don't know how old I am. What is a birthday? I don't think I have one of those." The little girl smiled.

Franke felt a rush of sympathy for the child who had never known the simple joys of a birthday celebration.

"Where are your mummy and daddy? Where is home?"

Keterlyn appeared deep in thought then said in a sad voice "I don't know where they are."

Franke smiled and tapped her hand on their clasped ones. "Don't worry. We'll find them. But do you at least know where you live?"

Keterlyn became animated, squeezing Franke's hand. "I can show you," she said, jumping down from the bed.

Still holding the girl's hand, Franke thought she was going to point to somewhere on the world map on the wall. Instead Keterlyn picked up her blue stone in her spare hand. The rock began to glow.

"Don't let go," she said.

Franke was struck by a feeling of trepidation, one which was immediately justified as she found herself holding the girl's hand in what appeared to be a cave. It was illuminated by phosphorescent rocks and veins in the walls.

Stunned and frightened, Franke grasped the girl's arm with both hands. She could hear the sounds of men and dogs somewhere nearby.

"This is my home," said Keterlyn, unperturbed by the sudden change in location. "A lady from the village brings me food and water. She is my friend."

Letting go of the girl's arm with one hand, Franke reached out to touch the solid, cold wall, assuring herself it was real. "Where? How?"

In response Keterlyn raised her finger to her lips. "Don't speak," she said. "Think it. That way the bad men won't hear you. I don't like the bad men."

In her mind Franke carefully formed her next few words. "Can you hear me now? Where are we?"

"I am home. I live here."

Franke could not help but smile at the girl's confident response. Not only that, but they were also communicating telepathically, speaking to each other with their thoughts.

She began to take in her surroundings more thoroughly, the setting of this girl's home. There was no furniture visible, just an old, handmade cup sat on a large flat rock. In a corner was a pile of ashes from a recent fire. Franke shuddered as the horror and squalor of the reality of the place sank in.

Keterlyn moved to a nook the floor of which was covered with leaves and straw. She drew Franke with her.

"This is my bed," she said, sitting and pulling Franke down with her. "All mine. Very comfy."

Franke began to shake uncontrollably.

"Are you cold?" asked Keterlyn. "I can light a fire now the bad men are gone."

"What do the bad men want with you?"

"They want to burn me on the big fire because I am a witch."

Franke was startled, her thoughts racing. Surely the practice of burning witches, barbaric as it was, had stopped in the Middle Ages? Was someone trying to frighten the girl? It was a dreadful thing to say to such a young girl, but she seemed to accept it.

Whatever was happening, Franke had had quite enough of it. "Can you please take me back now?" she said.

"I must find Meow first. I left her here in the bed. She is so lazy sometimes."

Keterlyn pulled away from Franke's grasp and began searching through her leafy bedding. She soon produced a cat-shaped doll, made of cloth and stuffed with something. Holding it tight to her chest along with the blue stone, the little girl reached out her free hand to Franke who grasped it eagerly.

In an instant they were back in Room 226. Standing at the foot of the bed, Franke took in her surroundings and, assured that they really were back in the hospital, let out a sigh of relief.

Keterlyn let go of her hand, jumped onto the bed and began speaking softly to her cat doll. Realising she could no longer understand her young patient, Franke quickly took up her hand again.

"I am very tired now," said the girl, yawning.

"Yes you are," said the doctor, pulling the bedclothes up with her free hand. "You get some sleep little one and I'll be back to see you later. Is that okay? Will you be a good girl for me?"

Keterlyn nodded sleepily and snuggled down into the bed, the cat doll and stone firmly in her grasp. Franke tiptoed to the door. Closing the door behind her she took a deep, shuddering breath, then started as she realised she was not alone. A woman and man stood alongside her.

"Is that the little girl's room?" asked the woman. "You must be the Child Psychologist. I'm Detective Inspector Walsh," she added, holding out her hand. "Please call me Janet. And this is Doctor Tony Small. We found her in the woods yesterday."

"I was hoping you would turn up," said Franke, shaking their hands in turn. "Great timing. I'm Franke Schwartz-Freud, the resident Child Psychologist here at the Royal. Please call me Franke."

"How is the little one?" asked Tony as Franke ushered them away from the door.

"She's very tired and is sleeping. Come, let's find somewhere quiet to talk."

They began to walk down the corridor when Franke stopped to look into the Nurses' Station.

"Can you keep an eye on the girl in Room 226 please?" she said. "She needs to be watched at all times. Oh, and is there a camera in the room?"

"We know the drill, thank you," said the nurse, looking up from her paperwork. "Security has CCTV links in all the rooms. You'll need to check with them."

"Thank you. Please keep a close eye on her."

Franke continued down the corridor before coming to a door marked Psychology Department. She held it open so her visitors could enter. Inside was a neat and tidy office with a desk positioned in the middle of the room. Behind it was a comfortable-looking reclining chair, in front two armchairs.

"Please take a seat," said Franke, moving to the recliner. The desk itself bore just a closed laptop, a mouse and a phone.

"Excuse me a moment but this can't wait," she said, picking up the phone and dialling. "Hello, Security? This is Professor Schwartz-Freud from the second floor. Are all the cameras on this floor recording? Specifically in Room 226?" Holding the mouthpiece of the phone away from her she muttered "Please. Please, please."

Tony and Janet exchanged glances during the short pause.

"That's brilliant. Now there's a large box of donuts in it for you if you can get a copy of the recording of, say, the last two hours, to my office within the next ten minutes. I can't stress how urgent this is."

Once again the visitors looked at each other, this time somewhat puzzled.

"You, sir, are my new best friend. Quick as you can. Thank you."

Hanging up the phone, she looked at the two puzzled faces in front of her.

"Jesus H Christ! Hells, bells and buckets!" Franke inhaled deeply, smiling at her confused guests and using her arms to push away her stress. She took another deep breath.

"I'm sorry about that. What a day," she said. "Right then. Her name is Keterlyn. We don't know where she's from and, in fact, neither does she exactly. She has never had a birthday and she doesn't know how old she is."

"Who doesn't know how old they are or where they are from?" asked Tony.

"You haven't heard anything yet," Franke continued. "I speak fluent German, as does she, but we can't understand anything either of us says. And she doesn't speak English."

DI Walsh was clearly puzzled but she crossed her legs and settled back into the armchair to hear the tale.

"She lives in a cave. Yes, a cave, with leaves for bedding. And a woman from the village brings her food and water." Franke was getting excited as she told the girl's story. "Meanwhile there are bad men trying to catch her and burn her at the stake because – wait for this – because she's a witch! She says so herself."

Tony and Janet looked at each other and began to laugh. Then, as the implications of what they had just heard sank in, they stopped, just as suddenly.

"That would explain quite a few things," said Janet, leaning forwards in her chair.

"Such as all the readings Johnathan got," said Tony.

"And how she wasn't there one minute …"

"And was the next."

They were interrupted by a knock at the door. Franke stood and swiftly went to open it. A large security guard filled the doorway holding a CD in a jewel case.

Taking the CD Franke said, "Oh brilliant, thanks Roger. I'll drop off the donuts first thing tomorrow."

The guard left and Franke returned to sit at her desk, opening the laptop and firing it into life.

"Remember I said we couldn't understand each other? Well, when we held hands, we could communicate telepathically and understand each other perfectly." She put the CD into the laptop. "But only when we held hands. We must have made some kind of connection somehow."

Franke moved the mouse, altering things on the screen, before turning the laptop around so her guests could view it. She rose and came to their side of the desk so they could all watch the footage together.

The screen showed Franke and Keterlyn holding hands. Although the picture was grainy, it was still clear enough to make out what was happening.

"You see I'm talking but Keterlyn isn't saying anything. Her mouth isn't moving. She's talking to me telepathically." Franke pointed at the screen. "Look there! Watch the blue stone. It will start to glow."

The three eagerly watched the screen, waiting for what was coming.

"Right about ... now!"

The blue stone in the girl's hand began to pulsate with yellow light. Suddenly Franke and Keterlyn simply vanished.

Franke leapt to her feet, bounding about the room and began screaming.

"Yes! Yes! Yes!"

"What just happened?" asked Janet.

"Look that's us entering the room," said Tony. "No wonder it was empty. They had just vanished."

"But where did you go?" Janet asked Franke.

Franke paused before continuing.

"What would you say if I told you we teleported to her cave, retrieved her cat-doll thing and then teleported back here again?"

The two merely stared at her for a moment. Then Tony spoke.

"A couple of days ago I would have called you crazy but today I believe you."

Janet, watching the screen again, nodded her agreement. Franke pointed at the screen just as she and the girl re-appeared in the room, Keterlyn jumping into bed.

"Well that was easy," Franke said. "I thought I'd have to fight to convince you."

Tony and the DI looked up from the screen as the video ended.

"When I said we found her amongst the trees," said Janet, "what I meant was that we found her amongst one hundred and thirty other children hanging from trees in the wood. We couldn't touch them. They were like holograms. But suddenly, Keterlyn?…" She looked at Franke for confirmation of the pronunciation of the girl's name. "Keterlyn took a breath and became real. We got her down from the tree and sent her straight here."

There was a long pause as Franke digested the information.

"One hundred and thirty you say?" she said. "And I suppose they are still there?"

"Still hanging from their necks, feet and hands, exactly as we found them," said Tony. "We could do nothing for them. As far as we can tell they are all dead, just as Keterlyn, er, was."

"Did she say anything about these other children?" asked Janet.

"Well, after our field trip she was too tired to do anything much. I guess the teleporting must have taken a lot out of her," said Franke. She put her hand to her mouth. "My God, did I just say that? Teleportation."

She took the CD from the laptop and put it back in the jewel case.

"May I have that please?" asked Janet, holding out her hand. "I'm sure I don't need to tell you that we need to keep this confidential between the three of us."

Handing it over Franke said, "Who would believe it? Look I'm not sure how many rules I've broken talking about this case with you but I think we all need each other's help to understand what is going on here."

"You could be right Professor," said Tony. Looking at the DI he added, "And I'd like a copy of that too."

Janet clutched the case to her chest. "We'll talk about it." Taking to her feet she addressed Franke. "Thank you for this Professor and please try and find out as much as you can about the other children. We'll pop by again this evening and hopefully we can all speak to her then."

"That will be fine," said Franke.

They all shook hands and Janet and Tony headed out the door. As it closed they heard Franke let out a shriek of excitement. They couldn't help chuckling as they walked down the corridor.

9

A DARK BLUE BMW 525 quietly rolled down the dirt track, through the open five-bar gate and into the field. Upon reaching the Mobile Command Unit it came to a halt and DI Walsh emerged from the passenger side.

"You drive like an old man," she said, laughing and closing the door. "I'm surprised you get anywhere on time."

Tony, refusing to rise to the bait, got out of the car and locked it using his key fob.

"My God, Tony. Who's going to steal it with thirty coppers around?" she said with a smile.

"Coppers! Never trusted them, me," Tony replied, returning the smile.

Poking her tongue at him, Janet led the way around the Unit towards the sound of the Ghostdusters excitedly arguing amongst themselves. Johnathan appeared to be conducting a lecture.

"It has to be an echo of an actual event as it happened, in real time but from the past. Like a time-tunnel or something."

"You're just guessing," said Matté.

"But so are you," said Johnathan. "Nothing on the meters yet you still think you know everything." He spotted the approaching figures. "Yo Doc and my lady. You'll never guess what happened in there." He indicated the woods. "Load it again Jim Bob."

Jim Bob opened the viewfinder on the digital camera he was holding and began pressing buttons.

"Watch this you two," said Johnathan. "We recorded the lot."

"You mean I recorded the lot," said Jim Bob.

Johnathan snatched the camera from his hands. "Your only contribution was setting it up on the wrong tree in the first place," he said.

"Which is why we got the footage and not just hours of trees."

"Yes, okay," said Johnathan. "Shut up and sit down."

Jim Bob sat on one of the flight cases, a smug grin on his face.

Johnathan brought the camera to Tony and Janet, fast forwarding as he did so.

"Watch what happens in a minute."

Taking the camera from him, Tony held it so he and Janet could view it clearly. The footage showed the children in the trees. Suddenly a man appeared wearing brightly coloured clothing, somewhat in the style of a court jester.

He had a struggling child under one arm. With his free arm he threw a noosed rope over the branch of a nearby tree. He fastened the noose around the neck of the frantically writhing child and, with a well-rehearsed movement, he dropped her.

The girl fell with a jerk, desperate for breath and scrabbling at the rope around her neck. Eventually her arms dropped to her sides and she hung still and lifeless.

"Oh my God," said Janet. "That's awful. The poor thing."

"There's more," said Johnathan.

Tony and Janet were transfixed by a screen for a second time that day, not daring to look away for an instant. They saw the jester move towards the screen, staring into it and reaching out with a bloodied hand towards it.

The screen went dead.

"Whoa," said Tony. "He saw it. How can he see it?"

Johnathan was nodding excitedly.

"Yes, right. Spooky or what?" Johnathan turned to Janet. "There you go Inspector. You have video footage of the killer caught literally red handed. And it's a clear image too."

"But it's not real," said Janet. "None of it. How can we arrest a man that doesn't exist?"

"Yes, right?" said Johnathan, smiling from ear to ear. "A close encounter of the second kind and we got it all on camera."

He began excitedly hopping from one foot to another until Janet held up the CD from the hospital.

"Another one for you to look at," she said. "A close encounter of the fourth or fifth kind by your scale. Use the equipment in the Unit if you like but don't break anything."

"We were playing in there before you got here," said Johnathan, snatching the CD. He headed off for the Unit, hotly pursued by his colleagues. "Hope you don't mind," he shouted back over his shoulder.

Tony passed the camera to Janet.

"What do you make of that?" he asked.

"It's incredible. I wish I had evidence as good in all my cases. It doesn't ever get this good. Ever!"

Tony sat on the log by the spent fire and Janet joined him.

"What's our next move?" he asked.

"Up to you, I'm well out of my depth."

"If I'm honest, so am I."

The two sat, lost in thought.

They were disturbed by the sound of "Whoa!" in unison coming from the Ghostdusters. A moment later a repeated "Whoa!" this time considerably louder, followed by laughter as the Unit began to shake.

"We could take this to the girl and see what she has to say," began Tony. "But …"

"Yes, it's too much for a six-year-old to see."

"Then what? She's the key to all this. I just know it."

The Ghostdusters returned to join them, full of smiles and grins.

"Can you print me off a picture of him?" asked Janet, holding out the camera. "But just him. Cut out anything that a six-year-old shouldn't see."

"For you, my lady, anything," said Johnathan. As he took the camera from her hand, he allowed his fingers to linger on hers. "Already done, my lady."

Johnathan noted a look of concern on the Inspector's face but was unsure if it was a result of his attention being unwanted or simply that he was a step ahead of her.

"Here you go," he said, producing a sheaf of photos from a file. "Your printer's much better than ours and we got a bit carried away."

On top of the pile was an image of the killer looking straight into the camera.

"Oh, that one's perfect," said Tony. "He looks positively evil. Hang on."

"What is it?" asked Janet.

"There in his belt. What is that a stick or something?"

"You noticed it too," said Johnathan, giggling excitedly. "I missed it, but Matt spotted it. We had it enlarged," he said, pointing at the pile of photos.

Janet began to flick through the images.

"Near the very bottom, my lady," said Johnathan.

She put half the pile on the floor and leafed through a couple more before she came to the one she wanted. Handing the photo to Tony, she picked another almost identical one.

"It's a flute of some kind, isn't it?" she said.

"Yes. It looks like it's made of bone," said Tony.

Johnathan was getting excited again. "Your turn to dazzle them Matt."

Matté took the photo from Tony and held it to his chest so they could all see it.

"I did a little research into bone flutes and the colourful costume he's wearing." Matté jerked his thumb at the Command Unit. "You know that's a great set up in there. Where can I get one?"

Janet rolled her eyes.

"Anyway, I digest. These kinds of flutes have been in use for something like thirty-five thousand years. And that costume he's wearing dates from the thirteenth century."

Matté paused and looked at Johnathan. "Do you want to?"

"No," said Johnathan. "He's all yours. You found it."

"Okay then," Matté continued. "In 1284, and there is documented evidence to prove it, in Lower Saxony, which is in Germany, or at least it was. Anyway, a man dressed in a brightly coloured coat and hat played his flute and danced away with one hundred and thirty children. None were ever seen again."

"The Pied Piper of Hamelin," said Janet. "I remember the story. Wait a minute, are you saying …"

"He is the Pied Piper of Hamelin," said Johnathan, jabbing a finger at the photo. "And that," he added, pointing to the trees, "is what he did to the one hundred and thirty children who were never seen again."

Tony looked at the image, then at Janet and back to the photo again.

"Oh, come on," said Johnathan. "It has to be. We've got one hundred and thirty children and a piper of sorts. Pied means multi-coloured so that's his clothing accounted for. It has to be."

"We've got a little girl who speaks German that nobody can understand," said Janet, looking at Tony. "Maybe it's a regional dialect from thirteenth century

Germany? And in her own words she is a witch who can teleport and talk to people with her mind."

Johnathan had started bouncing on the spot again.

"It's not too much of a stretch, is it?" Janet continued. "Too many coincidences not to be."

Matté and Johnathan bent down to Tony's eye level, eyebrows raised in anticipation.

"You know what Matté?" Tony said. "I think you could be right."

The pair leapt into the air with shouts of joy.

"Way to go Matté," screamed Johnathan.

Matté took his hands and they bounced around cheering. Suddenly Matté stopped.

"Did you just give me an accent?" he said.

"Yes, because you deserve it," said Johnathan. They started their bouncing again before collapsing in a heap of giggles.

Jim-Bob slowly raised an arm and said, "Yay Ghostdusters," with little enthusiasm.

Tony stood, photos in one hand, key fob in the other.

"Let's get these pictures in front of the girl and see what she can confirm," he said.

"Good idea," said Janet, also standing. "But I'm driving. Maybe we can get there before supper." Snatching the key fob from his hand she strode off.

10

INSIDE ROOM 226 THE bedside table was now raised and across the bed. On it was a pile of paper and various thick coloured crayons, together with a propped-up cat doll, sitting and watching.

Keterlyn was eagerly scribbling on the paper, paying little mind as to what she drew but amazed by the process.

Franke entered the room and approached the bed. The little artist looked up and smiled before resuming her work. Pulling up a chair Franke seated herself by the bed and reached out to touch Keterlyn's hand. The little girl stopped and looked up. She picked up her blue stone from its hiding place and held up her closed hand for Franke to hold.

"I like your drawing," said Franke. "You are very good at it."

"I have never done it before, but I like it." The words appeared from nowhere in Franke's head.

"I would like you to meet two friends of mine. You have met them before. They are the nice people who helped you yesterday and sent you here to me."

The voice came again. "Will you stay with me too?"

"Of course, I will Keterlyn. Nobody is going to hurt you here."

Franke placed her hand on top of the little girl's.

"Can I fetch them in now?"

Keterlyn nodded her approval, so Franke went to the door and opened it, ushering in Tony and Janet.

"Come in my friends," said Franke before whispering "Hug me, show her we are good friends."

They hugged her in turn and moved into the room. Franke perched on the bed while Janet took the chair. Tony found another chair and seated himself between the two of them.

"You are looking much better, little one," he said. "How do you feel?"

Keterlyn gave Tony a puzzled look.

"Of course. You can't understand me."

The girl looked at Franke and indicated Tony. The voice came once more in Franke's head.

"I think you'd better hold his hand."

Franke held out her hand to Tony who, realising what was implied, moved his chair closer to her.

"You too Inspector," said Franke. "Take the Doctor's other hand."

Janet reached for Tony's hand and, as they touched for the first time, they smiled at each other. Tony started as a voice spoke in his head.

"I remember you."

He saw Keterlyn was looking directly at him.

"This is weird hearing you speak but not seeing you talk," he said.

"I heard it too," added Janet.

"Think it Doctor," said Franke. "You don't have to say it out loud. And we should all be careful of our thoughts."

"How are you feeling Keterlyn?" Janet's voice came into all their minds.

"I am well again, thank you," was the quaint reply.

"That's a nice picture you have drawn. What is it?"

"It's just a picture."

"You are very polite," continued Janet.

"I may be a witch, but I am a good girl too."

The three adults chuckled at the formality of the little girl. Keterlyn lifted the blue stone to her chest.

"That's a pretty stone," said Janet. "I like the colour. What is it?"

"It's my sky stone," said Keterlyn proudly. "A bit of the sky that fell in a big storm, just for me." The stone glowed in her hand.

"I have a picture too," said Tony. "I was hoping you might be able to tell me who it is. We know he is a very bad man, but we don't know his name."

He took the photo from his jacket pocket and passed it to Franke who held it steady on the table. Keterlyn became visibly agitated. The air around them seemed to get warmer and suddenly the photo burst into flames.

"Rattenfanger!" screamed a terrified Keterlyn.

There was a momentary panic as the adults saw the flaming photo light Keterlyn's drawings. Tony flicked the smouldering papers onto the floor where he and Janet stamped them out.

The girl had her face buried in Franke's arms. Tony reached out and took Franke's hand. He spoke in their heads.

"I'm sorry little one. He was a very bad man but now he's gone. I'm sorry if he frightened you."

Janet joined hands to be able to hear the conversation as Keterlyn looked up from Franke's arms.

"He is the rat catcher, a very bad man," thought Keterlyn. "He hurt my friends."

"Were those your friends with you in the trees?" asked Tony.

The little girl perked up becoming suddenly happy and excited all at once.

"My friends are here? Where are they? Can you take me to see them please?"

The three adults, holding hands, looked from one to another, wondering which one of them would be brave enough to break the news to the girl that all her friends were dead.

Everything went dark for an instant then they found themselves in sunlight, standing in the woods surrounded by bodies. Keterlyn let out a piercing scream at the sight of her friends hanging limp from the trees. Franke dropped Tony's hand and tried to cover the girl's eyes.

Then Tony and Janet were standing alone. Franke and Keterlyn had disappeared.

"I think this may have been my fault," said Tony. "I thought of this scene just before we arrived. Keterlyn must have seen it too."

"Don't blame yourself," said Janet. "I was thinking the same thing."

11

THEY BOTH LOOKED AROUND for the incline leading to the way out. Spotting it first, Janet dragged Tony towards it. Heading up the incline they came out of the woods expecting to see Johnathan and the boys. But there were no Ghostdusters and no Mobile Command Unit. Nor was there a field of knee-high grass with a dirt track running through it, leading to a farmhouse in the distance.

Puzzled, they looked at each other.

"Where are they?" said Janet.

"No, no," shouted Tony, running back towards the trees, quickly followed by Janet.

Tony went to the nearest child and slowly reached out a hand. He proceeded to touch another half dozen bodies.

"I think you mean *when* are we? I felt flesh. These poor kids are real."

The smell then hit them both like a sledgehammer. They turned and fled up the incline again, gagging despite clasping their hands over their faces. Janet came to a sudden halt as they left the trees causing Tony to bump into her. Immediately in front of her was a man dressed like a court jester with the limp body of a child in his arms.

He looked at her and his blood-spattered face formed into a grin revealing black and broken teeth.

"Boo!" he said.

Janet flinched and took a step back, falling to the ground as she tripped over a branch. He stepped closer, forcing Janet to use her feet and elbows to scramble away from him.

"Tony," she cried, looking around for him. He was not there.

The man pressed nearer, then stopped. A confused look came over his face. He dropped to his knees and fell face down on the ground, the child still in his arms. Tony was revealed standing directly behind him, a thick branch in his hands.

Janet took several deep breaths and a wave of relief wracked her body.

"For a Detective Inspector you're awfully skittish, you know," said Tony, smiling.

Janet slumped back into a pile of leaves, returning his smile.

"Jesus Tony. I thought you were behind me."

"I was. Right up until you fell over. I ducked behind a big oak and waited for you both to pass. Then I grabbed the only thing I could find and encouraged mister serial killer here to cease and desist."

"Well, he stopped alright. I thought he was going to kill me."

Tony dropped the branch and reached out a hand to Janet. Taking it, she hauled herself up and dusted herself down. She looked at her fallen adversary.

"We'd better tie him up or something," she said. "He won't be too happy when he wakes up. We'd better check the girl too."

"I'm sorry, I didn't give her a thought," said Tony. "I was only thinking of you."

"Oh, that's sweet."

"You know what I mean."

"Don't ruin it for me, Tony."

They lifted the man off the child and Tony checked her for a pulse.

"She's alive," he said, relieved. "I can't tell if she broke anything in the fall, but I guess we'll find out when she wakes."

"Let's get this maniac tied up. Are you wearing a belt Tony?"

"No, I'm the same size now as when I was fifteen."

"Well, aren't you the lucky one. We'll need something."

They looked around.

"Wait a minute. What was he going to hang her from a tree with?" said Tony as he began to search the Piper's body. "Got it. Under his tunic."

Tony pulled out a length of rope and quickly tied the Piper's hands securely behind his back.

"You've clearly done that before," said Janet. "Should I be worried?" She raised an eyebrow.

"Ha no! I did one of those outward-bound wrangling courses with some students from a school I used to teach at. Surprising what you remember when you need to."

"Poor thing," said Janet, brushing dirt from the girl's face. "I bet she was petrified. Can you imagine how scared she must have been? Tony?"

The doctor was lost in thought, looking down at their captive.

"Are you okay Tony?" She reached out and gently touched his arm.

"You know I think we have a bigger problem," he said.

"What's bigger than being trapped here?" she snapped. "Illegal aliens stuck in a foreign country during the Middle Ages. Bigger? Really?"

"Well, yes, actually. Are you a science fiction fan Janet?"

"What the hell has that got to do with anything?"

"Just hear me out. I watch a lot of sci-fi to know that some of it is based on science fact, albeit somewhat loosely. But bits of it is, none the less, factual."

"What are you going on about Tony?"

"The more I think about it, the more it makes sense. We shouldn't be here."

"No shit Sherlock."

"If we've travelled back in time we may have already messed around with the timeline."

"The timeline?"

"That's what they call it in sci-fi movies, Janet. A fixed line of events that have happened and are going to happen. Our being here could drastically affect that timeline."

"I still don't get it."

Tony grabbed a twig and, brushing leaves away with his foot, drew a line with it in the earth.

"I'm not going to profess to know all there is to know about this stuff but as I understand it there is a fixed line of time. One end is the past, the other end the future." He pointed to either end of the line. "If something different happens in the middle here, the future may go off in a different direction." He drew a line converging from the first. "So, the longer we stay here the more chance there is that we will affect what is supposed to happen."

"So, is it bad that a serial killer gets caught and a little girl lives?" asked Janet.

Tony was getting agitated. "It's more than just that. Who's to say that the descendants of this girl become … oh I don't know. What if they help Hitler change the course of World War Two and achieve his vision of world domination? Imagine if the Germans had won the war?"

Janet looked worried as Tony continued.

"What if stopping the Pied Piper today means that he doesn't go home and make love to his woman who then conceives the ancestor of Marie Curie or Einstein?"

He hurled the stick back amongst the trees.

"Okay Tony, I get it. We do nothing and say nothing to anyone."

"It's already too late," he said, pointing at the Piper. "We've already interfered."

"Then we need to get out of here fast."

"That's right Janet. Here hop into my time machine and I'll have us home for tea."

"Calm Down, Mr Negative, and let's think of a way out of here." She took him by the elbow. "We need to be positive. There must be a way. I know you can do it."

"There is only one way out of here and that's the way we came."

"So, the only way out of here is Keterlyn. She has to bring us home."

"Shall I ask her, or will you?"

"Oh, for god's sake, Tony! Lighten up."

Grabbing his jacket she pulled him towards her, kissing him passionately on the lips. Tony embraced her, returning the kiss. After a moment their lips parted but they still held each other.

"Better?" she asked.

"Oh yes."

"I'm sorry Tony but I've been wanting to do that since yesterday. You're slower than you drive."

"Well, I mean it was alright."

Janet hit him in the ribs. She smiled.

"Now just get us out of here."

"Okay I'm thinking. Don't hit me again."

He put an arm out and lent on a tree, chin in hand.

"Assuming that we haven't changed anything already, then hopefully Johnathan and the boys will still be watching."

"Yes, watching with the camera," said Janet. "So, they can see us! That's brilliant. Do you remember which way the camera was facing?"

"No, it all looks so different here."

"If I remember rightly, the camera was facing into the woods from the left of the clearing."

Janet moved to where she thought the camera would be, opening her arms in a V-shape as she did so.

"We need to be somewhere in that area if they are to see. If the camera is even still running."

"If I know Johnathan there are probably a couple more by now."

"So, they should see us," said Janet.

"Yes. Provided we are in the right place, they are still watching and we haven't already altered the timeline."

"Enough with the negativity. I'm surprised you manage to get out of bed in the morning."

"I'm not being negative. I'm a realist. I just don't want to build our hopes up about something that may not happen."

"Well I think – no, I know – that Johnathan is going to see us and we are getting back home."

"Good for you and I honestly hope you are right," said Tony. "But we need to face reality. We could be here for quite some time. Maybe the rest of our lives."

12

ALTHOUGH THE NIGHT HADN'T been particularly cold, the dew had soaked the ground like a sudden shower. The branches of the trees weighed heavy under the sodden leaves combining with the knee-high grass in the field to give the landscape a new, fresh look.

Johnathan hammered on the Mobile Command Unit's door, Matté at his side.

"My lady. Are you awake?" He knocked again. "We're coming in my lady."

"We need you to put your knickers on," Matté sniggered.

"Now Matté, not only is that totally inappropriate it is also utterly not true. She doesn't have to put her knickers on."

They burst out giggling like schoolboys in their first sex education lesson. Johnathan thrust open the door, hoping to catch the Inspector in a state of undress. To the boy's disappointment, they soon realised the Unit was empty.

"Sod it, she's not here," said Johnathan. "Oh well. Time to play."

Meanwhile Jim Bob was taking his turn in the wooded area. And he'd found something he wasn't expecting.

He made his way to the MCU and slapped on its side.

"Hey you guys. Get out here."

He turned and started back to the woods as the other two came out to join him.

"Now let's not get above our station captain," said Johnathan, catching up with him.

"Don't look at me. Look at them." Jim Bob pointed to the woods. "They weren't there yesterday."

"Who is that?" asked Matté, squinting and wiping condensation from his glasses.

"How the hell did they get there?" said Johnathan, moving in for a closer look.

Putting his glasses back on, Matté sprinted into the woods until he came to the bodies of Tony and Janet. Putting his hand out to shake them awake, Matté recoiled as his hand passed straight through them.

"Oh, spooky!" he said. "How are they doing that?"

"Captain, go and rewind the camera," said Johnathan to Jim Bob. "See if you can spot them arriving here for the first time. Did they walk in or what? It may give us a clue as to what's going on." He looked back at the image of the pair. "Trust the Doc to keep it to himself."

Jim Bob ran to retrieve the camera and take it back to the Unit.

"Matté go and get the gear," said Johnathan. "We'll need to take some fresh readings."

Matté headed off to the hearse and soon returned carrying the two flight cases.

"Are they back with the Pied Piper?" he asked.

"Looks like it," said Johnathan, pointing. "They seem to have done something to him. That's him tied up over there."

"Way to go Doctor Small," cheered Matté. "One bad guy in custody."

Johnathan began retrieving equipment from one of the cases.

"But what's going on and how did they get there?" he asked.

"And have they done it yet," added Matté with another snigger. "Look, they're cuddling."

Tony sat with his back against a tree at the edge of the clearing with Janet lying on his shoulder. Both were asleep. The Pied Piper began to grunt and groan, waking Tony who looked about him as he regained his faculties.

"Hey Janet," he said, gently shaking her arm. "Janet," he said again, careful not to attract the attention of their captive.

She woke with a start, pulling herself away from him as she did so.

"What's the matter?" she said. "And what time is it?"

"It's early and we need to wake up. Someone else is stirring," he added, pointing at the prisoner.

Janet looked at where the Piper lay, growling and writhing in his bindings.

"Does he seem angry to you?" she said.

"Wouldn't you be?"

"Can he get free?"

"Hopefully not, unless we untie him. I'm not sure how strong thirteenth century rope is but it should hold him." Tony got to his feet. "And the little girl's gone too. She must have sneaked off at first light. At least she'd recovered enough from her ordeal to get away from here."

"Maybe we should get away from here too."

"I could always knock him out again," said Tony, swinging an imaginary branch.

"We can't keep him tied up forever," said Janet, slapping his leg as she stood up.

"Ow. Come on, let's get out of here. Johnathan should have seen us by now if he's ever going to. This place gives me the creeps."

"Tony, do you think Johnathan and the boys have seen us? Will Franke be able to get the girl to come and get us?"

"I honestly don't know. But we'll find a way to get home somehow, I promise you."

Tony kissed her on the forehead and put his arm around her.

"But first things first," he said. "We need to find some food and water. I'm starving. Then we can decide what to do with his nibs over there."

"I thought you'd never ask. Okay, you Tarzan, me Jane."

They headed up the incline and out of the wood. They had only gone another ten feet or so when a wave of static electricity swept over their bodies, causing the hairs on their arms and legs to stand up.

"What was that?" said Janet, rubbing her arms.

"I don't know," said Tony, looking around. "But the wood has gone. Look."

"How can that be?" asked Janet.

Tony took a few steps back and disappeared from Janet's view. A moment later he reappeared, his hair standing on end causing Janet to burst out laughing until he ruffled it back into place.

"It must be some kind of force field," he said. "Maybe the Piper has more magic in him than anyone guessed. That would explain why the children vanished and were never seen again."

"Yes, it would."

Tony's stomach gave a sudden grumble.

"I'm hungry," he said. "Come on."

"Do you think there's a MacDonald's around here?"

They both laughed. Tony took her hand and led her from the field towards another. This one had what seemed to be a cultivated crop in it.

"What is it?" said Janet.

"Don't think it is wheat or barley," replied Tony, spying a group of mud huts with straw roofs nearby. "Quick, down behind this bush."

"What kind of girl do you think I am?"

The pair crouched behind the bush.

"We can't be seen," said Tony. "We can't risk it."

"Oh, not your timeline thing again."

"I just think if we are going to sneak into that village and steal their food, we ought to keep a low profile," he said, pointing at the huts.

"Well why didn't you say so?"

"I'd have thought it would have been pretty obvious to a copper."

Shouts were coming from the village and a group of men emerged carrying pitchforks and other farm implements. They were headed towards the woods, led by a little girl.

Janet popped up to take a quick look.

"Isn't that the girl the Pied Piper had yesterday? She must have told mummy and daddy. What do we do now?"

"Nothing. We just keep out of sight."

"But didn't you say we had to maintain your timeline or risk changing the future?"

"I know but we can't do anything about that now. And who's to say we won't get the blame if we're caught?"

"Oh yes, I never thought of that. Well maybe the Piper is supposed to be found tied up at the scene of the crime. Perhaps he disappeared because the villagers killed him."

"Shh. Keep down and keep quiet," said Tony.

The villagers passed them by, at least a hundred yards away. A little while after a solitary female figure left the village heading in the opposite direction.

"I wonder why she's sneaking out?" said Tony. "And what's she carrying?"

"If it's food we could run after her and you could knock her out so we could steal it."

"I can see why you took the honest route in life Janet."

"I resemble that remark. Wait a minute, though. Didn't Franke say that a woman from the village used to bring food to Keterlyn?"

"It could be bread wrapped up in a cloth and that's a jug of some kind. Let's follow and see where she goes. We can't stay here forever."

They followed the woman as she crossed a field and entered a clump of trees at the foot of a rocky crag. Coming to a large tree in a clearing she set down a round loaf of bread and a wooden jug. They spied an opening in the rocks at the foot of the crag as she looked all around her and called out something they couldn't understand. After a moment or two she set off back the way she had come.

"Talk about luck," said Janet, starting to move. Tony held her back.

"Wait a little longer," he said.

A few minutes later they were tucking into the bread and sharing the jug of water, enjoying their good fortune.

"Better than MacDonald's!" said Tony with a smile.

Janet scowled at him, her mouth full.

13

FRANKE AND A NURSE were standing over the sleeping girl.

"Poor little thing cried herself to sleep," said the nurse. "What happened to her?"

"It's a bit of a weird story, I'm afraid, and I'm still trying to get to the bottom of it. Did you sedate her?"

"No the poor little mite was exhausted. Sobbed quietly and calmly for twenty minutes or so and then fell fast asleep."

"So she's been asleep all night?" asked Franke.

"Yes, hasn't stirred bless her."

"Well I'm glad someone did. I was up all night worrying about her. I'm going to have to wake her now so you can go. I'll take over."

The nurse left the room as Franke turned her attention to the girl.

"Keterlyn. Keterlyn."

The girl woke with a start and pushed her back against the wall, pressing the blue stone to her chest. Realising it was Franke who woke her, Keterlyn spoke, then held out her hand. Franke took her hand.

"It's okay little one. You're safe."

Keterlyn began to cry and reached out her arms. Franke obliged with a hug. After a few moments sobbing, Keterlyn spoke.

"Are my friends in the sky now?" she asked, tears running down her cheeks.

"Yes, and they are playing together and they are happy. Don't feel sad for them. I know you will miss them. We all miss our friends."

Keterlyn managed a smile.

"Are they really happy now? No more hurt?"

"No more hurt for them I promise," said Franke.

"Then I will not be sad. But I will miss my friends."

Franke found herself wiping a tear or two from her own face.

"Do you remember my friends, Tony and Janet?" she said. "They came to visit you yesterday and helped us. Do you remember?"

Keterlyn nodded.

"Do you remember you used your magic to take us to that dreadful place in the trees?"

A look of horror crept over the girl's face.

"It's okay," said Franke quickly. "You're safe now."

"Are your friends in the sky now?"

"No but they need your help. Will you help them so they don't end up in the sky?"

"But they will be happy in the sky," said Keterlyn. "You said so."

"It's not the same."

"Why not?"

"Your friends had bad things done to them. It hurt them so much they had to go to the sky. They didn't have a choice. My friends, Tony and Janet, haven't had bad things done to them so they won't have to go the sky if we help them. Do you understand?"

Franke realised it was near impossible to make such concepts understandable to a six-year-old.

"How can I help them?" asked Keterlyn.

"We need to go back to the trees."

Keterlyn recoiled, pulling her hand away. Calmly Franke reached out and took her hand again.

"When we went to see your friends in the trees we came back without Tony and Janet. They are still there waiting for us to come and get them. We have to go back to help them get home."

"But I don't want to go."

"I know you don't. If there were any other way to bring them back, I would do it. But there isn't. You must take me there and bring them home again. It's the only way for them to get back."

Keterlyn looked sad.

"But I don't want to see my friends like that," she said.

Franke lifted the girl's chin so she could look her in the eyes.

"Okay. What if you took us back and kept your eyes closed? Could you do that?"

"I keep my eyes closed?"

"Yes, you can keep them closed."

"You won't let go of me, will you?"

"No, I won't let go. I promise."

In an instant they were gone.

Franke and Keterlyn appeared once more in the woods but this time it was different. All around them were villagers, crying and angry at the sight that greeted them. Some tried to pull children's bodies from the trees. Others were comforting the many overcome by grief.

For a minute or two Franke and the girl went unnoticed. Then a man shouted.

"Look! The little witch. She did this."

Somehow Franke was able to understand every word.

"Keterlyn I'm sorry but you have to open your eyes now."

Angry and hurt villagers began moving towards them.

Franke was on the verge of screaming now.

"Open your eyes!"

The girl did so, saw the mob and screamed. She raised a hand and a sudden gust of wind caught the villagers, pushing them back. Some hit trees, others fell to the floor.

Keterlyn fled, pulling Franke along with her. Leaving the wood they fled into a field until Franke, exhausted, had to stop, dropping Keterlyn's hand.

"Keterlyn wait. Stop."

She didn't though, running on instead.

Eventually Keterlyn came to another wooded area at the foot of a mountain. Inside a familiar friend stood in her way. It was a large deer, obviously in some pain. Keterlyn noticed the arrow embedded in its side and tried to calm it with gentle shushing noises.

She ran her hands down the back of the deer until she reached its wounded flank. Her hands began to glow and the deer shifted its balance uneasily. Keterlyn shushed the animal again before touching the arrow with a tiny fingertip. The wooden shaft immediately turned to ash and was blown away by the gentle breeze.

The girl opened her hand and saw the metal arrowhead lying there. She threw it into the undergrowth. Holding her glowing hands on the open wound, she watched calmly as the flesh healed and knitted back together.

The deer licked Keterlyn's face as though in thanks, causing her to laugh, before the animal sped off into the trees.

Franke took two deep breaths and ran after her. Eventually she came to another wooded area at the foot of a steep crag. As she entered the wood, she saw Keterlyn up ahead jump into Tony Small's arms. Franke's relief turned to horror as she saw the little girl reach out to put her arm around Janet's neck.

The three of them disappeared.

Franke could hear the voices of the villagers behind her getting louder. She moved through the woods to the foot of the crag and spotted a small opening. An idea came to her and she got down on all fours to crawl into the opening.

Inside it soon became possible to stand and she found herself in a chamber.

"Yes," she exclaimed. "This must be Keterlyn's home."

She looked around at the glowing veins in the rocks and leafy bedding.

"I'm here Keterlyn. Come and find me."

As if answering the call for help, Keterlyn materialised before her, looking near exhausted.

"Thank God," said Franke.

Keterlyn seized her hand.

"I said don't let go," she said sharply.

Franke smiled sheepishly. She felt a sudden shock as a hand grabbed her leg. Looking down she saw a man dressed in motley, just as the three of them disappeared from the cave.

Franke was already screaming when the three of them reappeared in the hospital room.

"Keterlyn stop! It's Rattenfanger."

Tony reacted first, pulling Keterlyn out of harm's way. She fell limp in his arms.

Meanwhile the Pied Piper leapt to his feet and pulled Franke towards him, using her as a human shield. As he gazed in amazement around the room, it was obvious he wanted to get away as quickly as possible.

Keterlyn had fainted and Tony laid her on the bed. As he did so the blue stone fell from her hand and he instinctively snatched it up, wondering if he could use it somehow. He held out the palm of his free hand towards the Piper.

"Go home," he said, clutching the stone to his chest as Keterlyn did.

Nothing happened.

The Piper growled something unintelligible, drawing Franke closer to him so she totally obscured his body.

"Do you have a gun, Janet?"

"No, I'm not Roy Rogers Tony."

"Oh for God's sake," said Franke. She pushed her backside into the Piper's groin, thrusting her head back into his face as hard as she could. Pushing away from him, she punched him, splaying his nose.

The Piper, taken totally by surprise, staggered back then lunged for her. A swift kick to the groin sent him to his knees. In a quick, fluid move he had his flute to his lips and a sweet melody filled the air.

***

Tony came around to find two nurses standing over him. As he looked around the room he saw Janet being taken away on a gurney by a porter and another nurse. Then he noticed the door.

It appeared to have been blown clean off its hinges and lay askew on the other side of the corridor. Bits of wood and brick covered the floor.

"What happened?" he asked.

"We don't know," replied one of the nurses. "Calm down and relax, sir. We've got you."

"Keterlyn. Is she okay?"

"Yes, looks like she slept through everything."

"What about Janet and Franke? Are they okay?"

"They seem a bit dazed and confused like yourself, sir, but everyone will be fine. Just relax while we get you sorted."

Tony tried to sit up but became dizzy and passed out, banging his head on the floor.

Several hours later he woke to find Janet standing by his bedside looking concerned.

"Oh Tony, thank God you're alright."

"I'm not alright. My head hurts, my back hurts and I've no idea what happened."

"You've had a concussion Tony. You've been out for hours."

"So what happened?"

"We're still not sure," replied Janet. "All we do know is that we have an angry Piper at large somewhere in Gloucester."

Tony gingerly felt the back of his head.

"What about the girl?"

"She's fine. Look, Tony, get some rest and we'll talk later."

"And Franke? Is she okay?"

Franke appeared at Janet's side.

"Yes I'm doing fine, thanks for asking. I got Roger to send another CD for us to look at when you're feeling better. Only his name's Simon now. Don't ask. We'll fill you in later. Oh and Janet told me all about the Pied Piper."

"What do you think?" said Tony.

"Two days ago I'd have laughed at how ridiculous it sounds. But now, well, I can believe it."

"Get yourself together and we'll be back in a bit," said Janet, gently patting Tony's hand.

"Okay, give me five minutes," said Tony as he tried to sit up. He let out a groan. "Better make that ten," he said, grimacing and holding the back of his head.

"There are some painkillers on the side there if you need them," said Janet as she and Franke left the room.

14

AN HOUR OR SO later Tony found himself in the corridor between Franke's office and Keterlyn's room. He was having difficulty locating Room 226. He checked the numbers on the doors and found 210, 212 all the way up to 220, which is where the corridor ended.

His head hurt and he was clearly confused when he heard Janet's voice.

"There you are Tony."

He turned to see Janet and Franke coming round the corner.

"We thought we might find you here," said Janet.

"Here. Where is here?" said Tony. "I thought the girl's room was 226 but I can't find it."

"Yes," said Franke. "We noticed that too."

"I must have hit my head harder than I thought."

"No you didn't, Tony," said Franke. "Come back to my office and we'll fill you in."

"Lead on. I don't expect I could find it anyway."

The office seemed a lot further away than it should have been but at least the door was in the right place. Franke held it open. Forgetting his manners, Tony marched in and sat down before the women, his head in his hands.

"Why couldn't I find the girl's room?" he asked.

"You did," said Janet, sitting in the chair next to him. "Only now it is Room 212."

"Oh, you moved her because of the mess."

"No there was no spare room to move her to," said Janet. "They repaired the door and she's in the same room she always was."

"We all thought it was Room 226," said Franke, perching herself on the desk in front of them.

"If my head didn't hurt so much already I'd say it was beginning to right now," said Tony. "From the beginning please."

"You were right about the timeline thing Tony," said Janet. "There have been changes to this timeline now. Subtle changes perhaps but enough to make us realise things are not the same."

"It's fantastic really," said Franke, "And nobody seems to have noticed the changes apart from us. It's as though it has always been this way for everyone else."

"What sort of changes?"

"Not so loud Tony," said Franke. "You remember Roger, the big security guard who brought us the surveillance CD from Keterlyn's room the first time we disappeared?"

"Yes, of course," said Tony.

"Well he's Simon now."

"What? And why are we whispering?"

"Because anyone hearing us will think we're raving lunatics," said Janet.

"Not a good term to use in a Psychiatric Ward, Janet," said Franke.

"Sorry."

"Roger is now called Simon and he thought I was joking when I kept calling him Roger. He has been called Simon all his life and was getting quite annoyed before I dropped the subject."

"I was afraid of this," said Tony. "Didn't I say so, Janet, eight hundred years ago?" He started to laugh then stopped, holding his hand to his head.

"Serves you right," said Janet, smiling and slapping his arm. "This is serious. I phoned your office to let them know you were okay. No Professor Williams has worked there during the twenty odd years Deborah has been Chancellor."

"Who the hell is Deborah?"

"Exactly. It gets worse." Janet paused. "She didn't know who you were. This is getting way too confusing for me."

Tony stood and began pacing.

"The first thing is not to be panicked by this," he said. "We need to slow down a bit and I need to get out of this hospital."

"Tony," said Janet, just a little too loudly. "Stop with the jokes."

"I will if you'll be truly honest with me. Are you being serious or just taking advantage because I've got a bad head?"

The reaction from the women drained the smile from Tony's face.

"You are serious," he said. "I'm sorry. I get it now."

Tony stopped to look out of the window, to try and spot any more changes in the real world.

'The real world.' Was any of this real or would he wake up in the middle of a bad dream? Had he really been knocked out by an eight-hundred-year-old villain whilst trying to save an eight-hundred year old six year old? The more he thought about it the more confused he got.

He turned to face the others.

"The Piper. This Piped Piper. Does he exist? Was all that real?"

"Yes," said Janet. "And he is at large here and now, in this time, somewhere in the middle of Gloucester."

Franke spoke. "We have CD footage of what happened in Room 212 thanks to Roger. I mean Simon."

"Well let's see it then," said Tony. "It's as good a place to start as anywhere."

Franke opened the laptop, put the CD in and pressed play. The three of them sat watching the screen. There was nothing, just a screen filled with numerous white dots like a snowstorm.

"It can't be blank," said Tony. "That room, be it 226 or 212, has always existed, so there must be something. What about the debris and the broken door?"

"What can I say?" said Franke. "That's all the footage that Security has."

She rewound the video to little effect.

"Damn it," said Tony. "I can't remember everything that happened. I was hoping to see something."

"Stop!" said Janet. "Look."

There appeared to be images on the screen. Franke pressed play and Tony and Janet appeared on the screen, back in the room.

"You had it too far forward," said Tony. "That's us waiting for you to come back."

Keterlyn, Franke and the Piper suddenly appeared and instantly the screen turned to snow again.

"That's weird," said Franke.

For the next twenty minutes they rewound the CD to an hour or so before the appearance of the three of them. Then they moved the CD forward in short bursts. It left them none the wiser.

"Damn it," said Tony. "Let's go and see Keterlyn and see if she can help."

"That's another problem," said Franke.

"What do you mean? Is she alright?"

"You'd best come and see for yourself."

The three made their way to Room 212. Franke knocked and opened the door. They could see Keterlyn where they had left her, laying on her bed. But now she was encased in some sort of fuzzy bubble. Tony went in, only to be confronted by a security guard.

"It's okay Brian," said Franke. "Andrew, Graham. Peter?"

"Still not even close Sarah, Janet or Jane," said the guard with a smile.

Franke blushed. "Could you wait outside please?"

Waiting until he had left, Franke turned to meet Tony's puzzled look.

"I've had to turn it into a game," she said. "I'm supposed to have known them for years but I can't get any of their names right. Their new ones, that is."

"I'm impressed," said Tony.

"Yes I seem to have a bit more pull in this place since our little adventure. I've managed to keep this pretty quiet."

Tony turned to look at Keterlyn. She appeared to be asleep but he couldn't be certain. He reached out to touch the bubble.

"Don't Tony," said Janet.

He touched it anyway then jerked back as a force like an electric shock ran up his arm.

"Damn it!" said Tony. "What a day I'm having."

Janet smiled and, noticing, he bumped shoulders with her.

"You could have warned me a bit quicker, Janet. Has she been like this ever since?"

"Yes and we just don't understand it," said Janet, pointing at the bubble.

"We think she did it to protect herself," said Franke. "A sort of last resort."

"We also thought her blue stone might be able to burst the bubble, so to speak," added Janet. "But we can't find it. She must have it with her in there. But the longer she is in there the loner she goes without food and water and the weaker she will become."

"Wait a minute," said Tony. "I took the stone from her, hoping to use it against the Piper somehow." He began searching his pockets. "I definitely had it when I put her onto the bed."

Tony started searching the room before pulling up short.

"Of course Housekeeping would have tidied the room by now, so if I had dropped it they would have taken it. It's probably in a furnace by now."

"Ah, there's Mister Negative again," said Janet.

Tony dropped to his knees, first looking under the bedside table, then under the bed.

"Ah, there it is," he said. "But I don't see how it helps us. That force field goes through the bed right down to the floor."

The two women got down to see what Tony was referring to. Sure enough the static bubble went to the floor. Just inside it, resting against the skirting board, was the glowing stone.

Tony stood, hand going once more to his head.

"Well that blows your theory anyway, Janet. The stone is having no effect on the bubble. Nothing happened when I tried to use it on the Piper either so it must be symbiotic with the girl."

"What does that mean Einstein?" asked Janet, as she and Franke got to their feet.

"The two things, the girl and the stone, are ineffective on their own. Either they only work when they are in contact with each other, or it is all down to her."

"So what can we do to help her?" asked Franke.

"I'm not sure we can. Maybe things will reset when she recovers or has enough sleep or whatever. I don't know. And my head still hurts."

"Well she's safe for now," said Franke. "Let's leave Tony to get some rest and finally get rid of that headache. Then we can get together and brainstorm. There's a couch in my room if you want to get your head down Tony."

"Is there?"

"There is in this timeline."

Tony muttered a soft curse.

15

NOT MANY, IF INDEED any, members of the British public realise there is an English contingent of the American Security Services. Regardless of whether you knew it or not, there he was, standing alone, waiting in the shadows. Waiting in the dark and damp where the noise was way too high for his aged ears.

Lead Investigator Arnold Fitch was in his fifties and stood around six foot tall, dressed in the company cliché uniform of black suit, white shirt and black tie. He was one of the few long timers at the Department who legitimately held multiple passports, both English and American. They rarely took him Stateside these days since that incident three years ago. He didn't like to think about that.

Fitch was one of the stereotypical Men in Black as it was always his job to look into unusual occurrences in the UK. If anything out of the ordinary happened there and the States wanted to know about it, Fitch was their man. So far they hadn't noticed anything strange taking place in Gloucestershire but that was soon to change.

Meanwhile Fitch's time was mostly spent going over cold cases. Sometimes it was hard for the Americans to work out what was just a peculiar class custom or ancient tradition as opposed to an unnatural event. Consider cheese rolling, cow tipping or dancing naked around the boulders at Stonehenge.

Today was not a good one for Fitch, cold and tired and stuck in the basement boiler room of the Gloucester Royal Hospital. He was waiting for Mr Shallow Pockets to turn up. He was a low-level informant who had seen too many spy films and expected to be paid an inordinate amount for information which inevitably proved to be as useful as what the English would call a chocolate teapot.

There was a loud metallic bang off to the left as a door was closed. Fitch blended into the shadows and waited. Soon enough Shallow Pockets appeared. He was a thin, scruffy hospital porter clutching a supermarket shopping bag.

"Mr Fitch? Are you there?"

Fitch stepped from the shadows, startling the young man.

"What have you got for me this time?" said Fitch.

"It's a doozie Mr Fitch. I told you I wasn't wasting your time. Honest I ain't." He handed Fitch the plastic bag.

Fitch looked inside. "Dirty laundry? What am I supposed to do with dirty laundry?"

"If you were a clever G-man you'd get it carbon dated. I think you'll find it comes from the thirteen hundreds. Then, when you know I'm right and have given me my ten grand, I'll tell you how it came to be in my hands, in perfect condition no less, eight hundred years later."

Fitch grabbed the porter by the arm and dragged him in so they were face to face.

"If you're wasting my time, kid, you'll be found in this bag in such a condition even your own mother wouldn't recognise you. Do you understand me?"

Fitch released him, pushing the bag back into his hands. The porter backed off a couple of steps. It was a common technique for Fitch who believed that if his informants feared him they were less likely to waste his time. He hated having his time wasted, another grudge against his employers for sending him to Britain to follow up trivial claims.

The porter scampered off, dropping the bag on the floor. Fitch bent down to pick it up, wincing as the effort triggered a sharp pain in his shoulder. The bullet wound was another reminder of his Stateside mistake.

"God I need a holiday," he muttered as he headed for the door.

16

JANET AND FRANKE OPENED the door and peered into the room like a couple of guilty schoolgirls. Tony lay on the couch with his eyes closed. He had been there for the last two hours trying to shake his headache. He realised that he should have stayed in A&E and let them help him but he was too concerned about Janet and the girl. Not that he would ever admit that. It was not his way.

But he had become very fond of Janet and she seemed to have feelings for him. She was so full of life.

"You awake Tony?" she called.

"Not sleeping, just resting," he said.

"How's the head?" asked Franke.

Tony sat up gingerly and found that the pain had subsided. A smile came to his lips.

"Houston, we have lift off," said Janet, matching his smile with one of her own.

Tony swivelled his neck, trying to ease the stiffness.

"What time is it?" he said.

"A little after seven," Janet replied.

"Is it just me or does anyone else feel jetlagged?" he said.

"We're fine, just a little tired," said Janet. "You did hit your head quite hard."

Tony began the slow process of getting to his feet.

"Any change in the girl?"

"No change," replied Franke. "Sorry."

"We need to decide what to do about the Piper," said Janet. "He can't be allowed to run free on the streets of Gloucester doing what he wants. What about the children?"

"Can't you put out an alert and let the boys in blue bring him in?" said Tony, finally standing.

"Unfortunately we have a chain of evidence to adhere to. He hasn't done anything wrong here. Yet."

"Well you're the Detective Inspector. What do you suggest?"

"Actually I'm a Detective Sergeant now and I've been ordered to take some time off to recover from the gas explosion."

"Gas explosion?"

"Yes that's the excuse to keep people away from the hospital," said Franke. "We're right above the morgue and it's happened before. So no awkward questions here, at least for now."

The three of them moved to the desk, Janet and Tony sitting in the armchairs, Franke perching on its edge.

"So what are we going to do?" asked Franke.

"We need to find him first before we can do anything," said Tony. "Where would you go if everything around you was scary and alien?"

"Familiar ground," said Janet. "A park or the woods." She reached out a hand and touched his, bringing another smile to his face.

"But we can't just go chasing after him," he said. "We need a plan. And we need to remember he has magic and we don't have Keterlyn to help us. We'll have to catch him by surprise so he doesn't see us coming."

"We can use the police," said Franke. "The hospital has done it before."

"What do you mean?" Asked Janet.

"We tell them he's an unstable mental patient who thinks he's the Pied Piper. He escaped during the confusion of the gas explosion. That way they will be looking for the Piper without knowing the whole story."

"You'll have to add that he's considered dangerous and the public shouldn't approach him," said Janet.

"Of course," said Franke. "Then when the police apprehend him nobody else will get hurt. I'll get right on it."

Franke picked up the phone. Tony and Janet moved to the couch so as not to disturb her. As Franke spoke urgently into the phone, Janet risked a quick kiss. Tony cuddled her in response.

"Are you honestly feeling better Tony or are you just being stubborn?"

"No, I'm much better now. That nap did me good. So what now? Just sit and wait until he's spotted?"

"We need to get Keterlyn back," said Janet. "Get her out of that force field somehow. We may need her help at some stage."

Franke's voice interrupted them.

"Yes, she was here," she said. "I'll see if I can find her." Covering the receiver with her hand, Franke spoke to Janet. "It's Detective Inspector Bush. I get the impression you're not supposed to be here."

"I'm not. Tell him I just popped in to check on the girl and I've left again."

Franke spoke into the phone again.

"Sorry you've just missed her. She came in to see the girl and has gone again. Sorry about that. Goodbye Inspector."

Franke hung up the phone.

"Does that mean you're off the case?"

"No, I'm supposed to be at home resting until tomorrow. Don't worry about him. Before all this I was his superior so I know how to handle him."

"What did he say about the Piper?" asked Tony.

"They've put out an all-points bulletin," said Franke. "If he's still around they should find him. I also said that he was originally found in woodland so hopefully they'll concentrate on parks and the like."

"Right let's go check on Keterlyn," said Tony.

"You've got a real soft spot for her haven't you?" said Janet.

"Let's just say she reminds me of someone I once knew. I wasn't able to protect her, but this time I am."

He headed for the door. The two women exchanged surprised looks before following him.

17

IN ROOM 212 TWO ghostly figures appeared at Keterlyn's bedside, one male and one female. They hovered just above the floor and were totally transparent, surrounded by a soft glow. Not a word passed between them. The female motioned for the male to reach out to the girl.

He reached into the static electrical force field, gathered the girl in his arms and took a step back. The female briefly searched Keterlyn's body, then closed her eyes and held out an open hand. The bed began to shake until the blue stone rose from under the bed and moved directly to her hand.

Clasping the stone tightly, the female waved her other hand through the force field, causing it to disperse. The two figures and Keterlyn abruptly disappeared.

Tony and the two women reached the door to Room 212 to find a security guard sat outside, almost asleep with boredom. Jerking alert, he smiled at them as they entered the room. A moment later they summoned him and he too entered.

Both the girl and the force field were gone.

"Where is she?" asked Franke.

"I don't know," said the guard. "She didn't come past me, I promise you."

"Go get some coffee and wake yourself up," said Franke. "Then get the video footage for this room for the last three hours and bring it to me in my office."

"She didn't come past me," he said as he turned to go.

"We believe you," said Franke. "Get some coffee and don't forget that CD."

An hour later they had watched the CD and established what had happened. Tony suggested that the ghostly figures might be Keterlyn's parents, but it was all supposition and guesswork.

"But what happens next?" asked Janet.

"That's what worries me," said Tony. "If we should happen to meet the Piper face to face, what do we do? How can we apprehend him? More importantly, without Keterlyns help, how can we send him back to his own time?"

"I guess we'll solve those problems when and if we meet them," said Franke with a resigned shrug of her shoulders.

18

The new forest, 1940

KETERLYN WOKE, STARTLED, IN unfamiliar surroundings. She lay in a bed she had never seen the likes of before, some kind of cage she imagined. She had never seen bunk beds. Looking around she could see she was in a house made of wood. It was dark and she could taste dampness in the air.

She whimpered, drawing the attention of a female figure sat at a wooden table faintly lit by a candle. The woman picked up the candle and moved towards Keterlyn. As she approached the candlelight made her features clearer and the girl soon recognised the blonde hair and blues eyes of her mother.

As soon as she was close enough, Keterlyn reached out and hugged her mother, burying herself into her body. She smelt the familiar lavender scent and relaxed into the warmth of the arms surrounding her.

Keterlyn began to speak but her mother looked confused, eventually holding up her hand to indicate she should stop. She reached under the girl's pillow to retrieve the glowing sky stone and placed it in Keterlyn's hand.

"Why did you leave me?" Keterlyn said. "I looked everywhere for you and I couldn't find my way home."

"We didn't leave you, my baby. As soon as you gained your powers you disappeared before we had the chance to show you how to control them. But we never gave up looking for you. We knew we'd find you one day."

They hugged each other for a long while before another approached them. He was tall with blonde hair and a beard that Keterlyn remembered playfully pulling on.

"Daddy," she said and he crouched, joining them in their embrace.

"Hello little one," he said. "Where have you been? We were so scared."

Over the next couple of hours Keterlyn recounted her adventures. They thought she may have been drawn to the thirteenth century by the old magic there, combined with the presence of witches. It was her misfortune to stumble across the Pied Piper.

Back here in the twentieth century magic is scarce and the old ways mostly forgotten. Had it been chance that Tanya Drinkwater had met her husband Luuk in the New Forest some fifteen years ago or had mystic forces been at work? Either way the girl from Devon and the big Dane had fallen in love and set up home.

Already seeped in lore and the old ways, they became proficient proponents of Wicca, the rites and casting of spells from the magic within oneself. They found it the best way to hide the fact that they had old magic which can be gifted from a dying witch to a chosen one or transferred via a talisman. Keterlyn's sky stone was such a talisman.

When Keterlyn had finally brought her tale to the modern day she declared herself famished and gorged on what her parents could supply. Unsurprisingly she became sleepy once more.

"You rest little one and we'll begin your learning in the morning," said Luuk. "I need to speak to the Magister and tell him we are now back to three."

Keterlyn was woken early the next morning. She had slept well and felt truly happy for the first time in a while. Smiling at her mother she stretched out her arms, shaking the remaining slumber from her body.

"Come on and get some breakfast sleepyhead," said her mother, indicating the table. "You've got a busy day today."

Keterlyn made her way to the table and sat on the nearest seat, her feet dangling above the floor.

"What would you like to eat for breakfast little one? There is some of your favourite here." Her mother held up a preserve jar with pink strawberry jam inside.

Keterlyn smiled and nodded her head, watching as a large slab was spread onto a doorstop of bread. She took it on the offered plate and a glass of fresh milk was put before her. She made short work of both.

"Steady on poppet. No-one is chasing you here."

Keterlyn talked for a minute or two in that strange language nobody understood.

After patiently hearing her out her mother said, "We'd best find your father and get you translated."

She opened the door, letting the morning sunshine stream into the dark cabin. Keterlyn followed her mother out into a clearing in the woods where her father was waiting for them.

He had prepared some lessons to help Keterlyn come to terms with the gift of her magic. She had been blessed with the gift by the old matriarch herself, Bethsheba. She was the last of the Semitic speaking Israelites and often spoke of the three kings, Saul, David and Solomon. Some said she was over three thousand years old.

Old magic high priestesses and coven matriarchs were said to live for thousands of years until modern magic found a way for greedy zealots to end the old magic for ever. As a result old magic was scarce as coven fought coven in a never-ending battle for supremacy.

This coven in the heart of the New Forest was the last of its kind, the last remaining bastion of old magic, the good magic. Keterlyn had been blessed by Bethsheba herself on her third birthday. Her frail young body could not be expected to contain the power of the magic granted to her so it had been transferred to a talisman. That was her sky stone.

As they entered the clearing Luuk greeted them.

"There you are. Did you sleep well little one?"

Keterlyn looked puzzled.

"Ah, of course. We need to hold hands," he said, thrusting a paw like hand towards his daughter. "Firstly, we need to combine yourself with the magic of the stone so no-one can steal the magic away from you. Then at least we'll sort this language problem."

He indicated to Keterlyn to sit on a nearby fallen log and beckoned Tanya to sit alongside her. Luuk took the blue stone from Keterlyn's hand and held it against her chest.

The stone began to glow, gently at first but soon a rhythmically pulsing light filled the clearing. It seemed to reach a crescendo then suddenly stopped. Luuk crouched down to Keterlyn's eye level.

"How does that feel?" he asked. "Can you understand me now?"

"Where is my sky stone?"

"It is inside you, little one," said Luuk. "It is part of you now and always will be. When you reach your full potential it will be no more. You truly are the blessed one."

"I can feel the Earth Mother," said Keterlyn. "She is happy now."

19

THE NEXT DAY HEAVY rain broke up the recent run of fine, sunny days. A typical English weather system was settling in bringing in rain for the next twenty-four hours. Or there may be sunny intervals, as they rarely seemed to get the forecast right these days. Whatever, there would be plenty for the Brits to complain about from under their umbrellas.

Tony hated the rain. He'd far sooner it be cold than wet. He had his only ever accident driving in the rain four years ago, taking his then wife Brenda and their six-year-old daughter Rebecca to the cinema.

It had been raining so hard his windscreen wipers could hardly keep pace when that idiot overtook and came at him on the wrong side of the road. Tony swerved off the road and collided with a lamppost. Luckily, he hadn't been going fast so nobody was hurt. Or so they thought.

About ten minutes later they realised Rebecca had impaled herself on one of her coloured pencils. She often drew pictures during long journeys. By the time the paramedics arrived it was too late. A total freak of an accident.

Things between Tony and Brenda were never the same after that. She blamed him for the accident and started drinking heavily. Then she announced that living with him was boring and moved to France to be with her parents.

The incident haunted Tony. Time and again he saw Rebecca in the faces of the schoolchildren he taught. Eventually he transferred to Higher Education to teach older kids who thought they were adults, even though they acted like kids.

Keterlyn reminded him of Rebecca. Carrying her tiny body from the tree the other day brought back so many memories. The smell of Rebecca's hair as he put her to bed after her bath and her tiny, mischievous smile.

A car horn jerked him back from his daydream, pulling the car back into the correct lane. That was stupid, he thought.

He hadn't slept much last night and it was probably madness to try and drive to the farm in this weather. But it was too late to turn back, he was almost there.

He pulled into the muddy drive and parked up in the boggy field next to Janet's car. As he was going to get out, he realised he had no wellingtons to put on over his smart street shoes. They would be ruined.

He was still sat there when Janet got in, her muddy boots making a mess of his carpet.

"Morning," she said. "Did you sleep at all last night Tony?"

"I couldn't get her out of my head, that's all."

"Keterlyn?"

"No, Rebecca." Tony seemed to come awake. "What's happening? Anything new?"

"It's all gone," said Janet with a sweep of her hand. "The kids, the ropes, everything. There's nothing to see any more."

"What do you mean all gone?"

"Just like the girl. Here one minute, gone the next. And my DI knows nothing about any of it." She took his hand. "I'm here if you want to talk, Tony."

"No thanks, not today." He didn't move his hand. "I was thinking on the way here, if I'm not working at the University, what am I supposed to be doing? And where are Johnathan and the boys?"

"They were nowhere to be seen. I assume they were never here either. Look, why don't you go home. I'll finish up here and meet you there later."

Tony nodded, she kissed him and got out of the car. He slammed the car into drive and wheel-span away.

20

PETER WALKER RUSHED INTO the forest clearing, looking for Luuk and Tanya. He was not so much a leader of their coven but more of a secretary for it. He took it upon himself to make sure everyone had everything they needed like clothes, food ration books and anything else. He was also the only resident of the forest that had access to a phone line and used it for everything official.

"Luuk, I have been looking for you both, Magister wants us all in the meeting room for something urgent."

"What, now? What could be that urgent?" Asked Tanya.

"I don't know," said Peter, "something to do with Prime Minister Churchill." Then rushed back towards the community areas.

"Churchill? Come on Tanya we better find out what's going on!" He crouched down and looked around to make sure his words were not overheard. "Now little one, I need to tell you something. You are a witch and Mummy and Daddy are witches too. We all have real magic powers. Those other people are Wicca. They do not have the old magic that we have and we must not let them know we have old magic. We must keep our powers hidden from them. Do you understand me?"

Keterlyn nodded. She took her mothers hand and they both followed Luuk out of the clearing. They made their way to the communal areas and could see people rushing into the large meeting room building. It was a basic design with log walls and wooden shingled roof, making full use of the resources available around them.

Inside the meeting room there was a lot of chatter and noise. Everyone seemed to be concerned as to why there was an unusual meeting being held today. Luuk, Tanya and Keterlyn took seats at the back of the room and waited for the magister to take the podium at the front. They didn't have to wait long before the magister entered and made his way down the centre isle towards the podium. He was dressed in animal furs and with a horned helmet not unlike a Viking. He was followed by his wife who liked to be called High Priestess. She wore a long white cotton robe adorned with various witches' jewels and of course the mandatory necklace. Upon reaching the podium the room fell silent and the aged face of the magister could be seen in the dimly lit room.

"Witches, Wizards, friends. We have been gifted a great mission to help with the war effort. A friend of mine who works for the secret service has asked on behalf of Prime Minister Churchill himself." He paused for the magnitude of his words to engulf his listeners. Surprised and excited faces filled the room, looking at each other.

"He has tasked us with the mission to send Adolf Hitler a message. We must tell Hitler not to cross the water and not to invade England."

An awe fell across the room.

"We have enough numbers among us to achieve this, but it will take every ounce of magical energy we have. We will start the ritual at sundown tonight, so get some rest."

Luuk took his family back to their cabin on the outskirts of the communal area, closing the door once all were inside.

"This could end bad," said Tanya. "A ritual of that size could take days and may never even achieve its goal."

"It could just be a way to discredit the coven and finally give everyone the chance to say magic doesn't work." Luuk pondered.

"But if we help, we could end up exposing ourselves to everyone else," Tanya pointed out. "Do you remember how the last big ritual seemed to pull magic from within us. I could hardly keep control then and this is going to be a much bigger spell. And what about Keterlyn, there is no way she could keep control yet."

Luuk walked to Keterlyn and crouched down in front of her. "Maybe we should all go on a little trip. Would you like to go to the seaside little one?"

Keterlyn smiled and knew it was going to be exciting even though she had never seen the sea before.

Luuk stood. "We will have to go now, while everyone is resting. Grab what we need."

Tanya grabbed a cloth and wrapped some bread and vegetables inside it. Luuk saw her.

"Really? Could we not just go old school." He opened his clenched fist and a bright red apple appeared in his hand. He gave it to Keterlyn. She held it in her hand, the apple split in two then she gave one half to her mother.

"Of course, we could, if we are careful." Placing the misshaped cloth back on the table. "Thank you, baby."

Keterlyn smiled and took a bite from the remaining piece of apple. Luuk opened the door of their cabin and there stood Paul Walker.

"Where are you going?" He asked.

Luuk waved his hand in front of Pauls face. "You are here to tell us that a phone call came for me, to tell me my mother is ill and to get back home as soon as I can. You told us and we left immediately. We apologised for not making the ritual."

Pauls face immediately changed and he agreed in earnest with Luuk. "Yes, you best get home she must be ill for them to call. Not sure how they got the number."

"We shall leave right away. Thank you, Paul, said Luuk.

Luuk took his wife's hand who was holding Keterlyn's and led them away from the cabin deep into the forest, heading towards the coast, towards Lymington.

21

AT THREE IN THE afternoon, Tony was woken by a banging on the front door. Pulling on his robe, he opened the door to find Janet stood there, a bottle in each hand.

"Didn't know if you were a red or white man so I brought both."

"Diet Coke man actually," Tony replied. "Can't drink that stuff anymore. It's addictive."

"Sorry," said Janet, stepping inside. "Do you mind if I do?"

"No, go ahead. I was going for a quick shower so make yourself at home."

He headed upstairs and into the bathroom. The shower had just warmed up when he was surprised to find Janet, naked, climbing into the cubicle beside him.

"What are you doing Janet?" he asked as she shut the glass door behind her.

"Making myself at home," she said, putting her arms around him and kissing him fully on the lips.

He responded, tentatively at first, but soon becoming more passionate. As the warm water caressed them, their bodies touched and pressed against each other and he could feel the tension washing away.

Tony wasn't someone who found it easy talking to women. Although not naturally shy, he became so when he had any purpose in mind. And he hadn't had such a purpose for some four years. Nevertheless, he more than made up for it that night.

They made love twice in the shower and twice more in bed, leaving them exhausted, out of breath and covered in sweat. Another shower would have to wait until morning, though.

As she lay next to Tony, watching him sleep, Janet wondered if he could be the one to fill the void she'd felt since her divorce from Simon. It had been a turbulent two years of marriage and it soon emerged that Simon saw her as just another conquest, despite his vows, and was soon moving onto another.

By the time the office gossip reached Janet's ears he was on his third or possibly fourth. As his superior in the force, she made sure he was kept busy and eventually secured a distant posting for him. It was then that she instigated divorce proceedings.

She saw Tony as someone gentle and caring but, like most men, needing help to share his feelings. Desperate to learn about Rebecca, she knew that he would tell her more eventually and that she just needed to be patient. But this new timeline had put a huge proverbial spanner in the works.

Before the change she had just had her two-bedroomed apartment in central Tewkesbury redecorated to her own taste. Now she was living in its undecorated state with Simon, who she found herself still married to. She was determined to get out of that situation as soon as possible.

Janet knew Tony had feelings for her and right now she had nowhere else to go. She might be using him, but that wasn't really her intention.

The buzzing of her phone interrupted her musings. Picking it up she retrieved and read the text. Janet immediately slapped Tony's backside through the covers.

"Tony! They've got him!"

"What's the matter?" he asked, rubbing the sleep from his eyes.

"They've got the Piper. They caught him in King's Stanley."

"Where the hell's that?"

"A village just a few miles away. Come on get up."

Janet kicked the covers off them onto the floor. Grumbling, Tony swung his legs out and stood up. Janet's phone pinged again.

"They've lost him," she said. It pinged again. "And they've got him again! What is going on down there?"

"Sod them. I'll put the kettle on," said Tony, retrieving his boxers and trousers and heading downstairs. "We'll go out for breakfast, providing they don't lose him again," he called out.

"Too late. They have."

Janet dressed quickly and joined Tony in the kitchen where he was making coffee.

"How can they find him and then lose him again within five minutes?" she asked.

"Maybe there's a problem with the network. What company are you with?"

"Virgin."

"Ah. It's bad for virgins around here."

"Yes," said Janet. "I've noticed."

"Oh, only in your wildest dreams were you a virgin," said Tony, smiling and passing her a coffee. "Of course, Simon could be experiencing the powers of the flute. That's something we couldn't warn him about."

"Yes, you're right. Come on, we need to get over there."

"But what can we do?" Tony sipped his coffee. "We haven't got a magic wand or any special powers to stop him."

"You don't want to?"

"Of course, I do. I don't want to let that monster loose. But I still remember our last encounter." Tony rubbed his temple.

"I agree, Tony. But I can't help thinking we're the only ones who can do anything. Only we know the whole story. Simon doesn't know he's a mass murderer. And to be honest that worries me. Someone could get hurt."

"Didn't you put him in your reports?"

"How could I? Explain that the real Pied Piper was brought back in time from 1284 by a six-year-old girl witch who was then abducted by her ghost parents? I'd be thrown off the force."

She finished her coffee in a single gulp. "Come on, I've worried myself enough now."

Grabbing coats and keys they headed out the door to her car.

"I'll text Simon to meet us there," said Janet.

Once they were in Janet's car they headed for King's Stanley and were there in thirty minutes. They pulled into the car park of the King's Head to find DI Simon Bush sat on the bonnet of his vintage Ford Escort.

Janet turned to Tony.

"There is one thing I haven't told you yet. Simon and I are still married."

"I thought you said you were divorced."

"We are. We were. Oh hell, you know how complicated thigs have got since we met Keterlyn. Before, when we met in the woods, Simon and I had been divorced for a year and he had moved out. But now, well that's all changed."

"That must have been a bit awkward for you," said Tony, who couldn't resist a chuckle.

They were both laughing as they got out of the car and moved towards DI Bush, standing with his hands on his hips, tapping his foot.

"Where have you been?" said Simon. "I waited up for you last night but you didn't come home."

"Nor will I ever again," said Janet. "It's over Simon. Deal with it."

"Maybe a DS in your position ought to be a little more careful."

"When you get the same results I do then I might worry about that," said Janet. "Until then, suck it up. Sir."

"And who the hell are you?" said Simon, turning to Tony.

"This is Dr Tony Small," said Janet. "He's a criminologist and, no matter how incompetent you feel, you should treat him with respect. Sir."

"You're quite right," said the DI. "My apologies Dr Small. Can I ask what your interest is in the case?"

"I am a lecturer from UWE and I've been observing and advising regarding this particular patient's behaviour."

Tony held out his hand and Simon shook it brusquely.

"Thanks for your help Doctor."

"I understand you've caught the fugitive," said Tony.

"We did but when we turned around he was gone. Not sure quite what happened. Anyway, what has all this got to do with the girl at the hospital? Or are we just doing favours again?"

"Not favours, Simon, our jobs," said Janet. "The fugitive has nothing to do with the girl. Where was he last seen?"

Tony was confused. What had Janet told Simon about Keterlyn? Did he know about the children in the trees? What actually *did* he know?

"He's got to be around here somewhere," said the DI. "Two officers reported him as caught an hour ago. Then we found them both here, alone and confused."

Tony glanced up at the pub sign.

"Drunk?" he asked.

"Anyone else and I might have doubted their stories but these are two reliable men. I believe them. But that doesn't explain what happened. He could have stolen a car and be miles away by now."

"No, I don't think so," said Janet. "The psychologist at the hospital, Franke, says he doesn't drive. In fact he hates all modern technology."

"Well now he has assaulted two of my men I've stepped things up. I've got ten men looking for him. If they spot him they have orders not to approach him but to radio in their position. We can then flood the area with more men."

"We'll attend as well to see if we can help out," said Janet. "Give me a call. We'll be in the pub."

"No, I'll be in the pub," said Simon. "You can join the search. I'm in charge, remember."

"Sorry sir. Of course, sir." Janet headed for her car. "Come on Tony, we'll drive round and see if we can spot him."

22

AGAIN, HE FOUND HIMSELF at the mercy of Shallow Pockets. What a stupid name, he thought. Another example of British humour he imagined. But nevertheless, here he was in the dank and dreary basement of the Royal, waiting for the porter to make his even later than ever appearance.

A metallic clang rang out above the noise of the boilers and Fitch knew this had to be him. About time too. He had better things to do than shadow hop in this God-forsaken hole.

He waited until the porter had passed him and had nowhere to turn before speaking.

"And what the hell time do you call this?"

"Did you check out the clothing? I said it would be worth your while, didn't I?"

Fitch did get the clothing carbon dated and it proved to be from the thirteenth century, exactly as promised. The state of the material was the most remarkable thing. Most cloth from that long ago would have deteriorated dramatically but, despite the ground in dirt and grime, this dress seemed to be in almost perfect condition.

"Where did you get it from Malcolm?"

"I told you not to use my name. And I ain't saying nothing 'till I get my money."

"If you're stringing me along, Malcolm ... well, let's just say you know what I'm capable of. And believe me I wouldn't lose any sleep over ending you."

The porter attempted to brazen it out.

"Show me the money, big guy, or I'm out of here."

Fitch stepped from the shadows, the bag clearly visible in one hand, a gun in the other. The porter reached for the bag and Fitch withdrew it.

"You give me the information and I'll give you the money."

"Show me the money I said and I'm not messing. For all I know that's just donuts in there or something."

Fitch raised the gun.

"I could waste you right here and no-one would be the wiser."

"I've had enough of this," said the porter, looking to head for the door.

Fitch stepped into his path.

"Okay. I've got the money."

Fitch holstered the gun inside his jacket and opened the bag, revealing its contents. Then he snapped it shut again.

"Money first," said Shallow Pockets, holding out his hand.

Fitch handed the bag over. The porter made a move for the door, only to be brought up short by a strong grip on his arm.

"Easy, big guy. Why don't you check out the little girl in Room 212? She owns the dress I gave you. And take a look at the CCTV coverage for that room for the last couple of days. Once you have, I'm sure you'll want to hand me over another ten grand."

"Is that it?" Fitch grabbed the man by the front of his boiler suit. "Is that all my ten grand gets me?"

"Look, if I could have got you the CCTV video I would have. I ain't got the clout. But I'm sure you'll be able to sort it."

"Listen to me, smart mouth. I'll check out the little girl and I'll watch the CCTV and if I find you're giving me a bum steer you'll wish we'd never met." Fitch had him on his tiptoes now, face an inch from his. "Anything else you want to tell me?"

"You got any breath mints?"

Fitch pushed him to the floor.

"Get lost kid."

The porter jumped to his feet, grabbed the bag, and made a dash for the door.

"And I know the number of your flat at Cherry Tree House if I need to find you."

The porter risked a final, anxious look at Fitch as he ran out of the door, clanging it shut behind him.

Fitch knew the kid was telling him the truth but it did no harm to keep him on edge. Informants needed to be kept in line and know that Fitch was in complete control.

He cupped his hand and breathed into it. A quick sniff told him he didn't need a mint after all.

"Bloody kids."

23

THEY HAD BEEN CRUISING the area of King's
Stanley, Stanley Downton and Leonard Stanley
for over an hour and were now on foot heading for
Middleyard and Selsley Common, checking various
barns and stables.

Tony's phone rang and he dug it out of his pocket.

"Tony Small," he said into it.

"Yo Tony! I've found you."

It was Johnathan.

"I didn't know I was lost."

"No dude. I mean where are you? We were supposed
to be checking out Longleat today. Remember?"

"Sorry, I forgot. I'm in King's Stanley today. Can
we sort Longleat tomorrow?"

"No can-do Doc. Lord Bath is angry we didn't turn
up yesterday so we'd better get down there. Why don't
I pick you up from your office in an hour?"

Tony wondered if he even had an office, let alone where it was.

"Why not pick me up from here," he said. "The King's Head in King's Stanley."

"Okay Doc. See you in an hour or so."

"Apparently I'm supposed to be in Longleat today with Johnathan," he said to Janet. "I'll have to leave you to it."

"No worries. There's nothing here so let's head back to the car. I'll drop you at the pub."

Tony grabbed her arm.

"Look down there," he said, pointing. "Behind that barn. It looks like him."

"I can't see anything."

"Down there, walking along the treeline."

Janet looked where he was pointing and saw a colourful figure ambling along a line of hardwoods.

"He's going to go out of sight behind that barn," said Tony. "We need a better view."

They quickly moved to another vantage point but to no avail.

"Dammit, we've lost him." Tony scanned the area but could find no sign.

"I'll call it in anyway. Let's get back to the car."

Janet spoke into her phone as they walked.

"We think we spotted him near Middleyard, sir. He was too far away to be certain. What do you want us to do? Okay, we're on our way."

Putting the phone back in her pocket, she turned to Tony.

"He seems angry at you for some reason."

"Me? What have I done?"

"Perhaps he found out I stayed with you last night instead of being at home with him. He is my husband after all."

"As if things weren't complicated enough."

The drive back to The King's Head was short and made in silence. Pulling into the car park they could see Simon pacing impatiently. As soon as they were out of the car he was addressing them.

"What's going on Janet?"

"Why, what's the matter now?"

"I've checked out your specialist here," he said, jabbing a finger at Tony. "He's not from the University. In fact, they've never heard of him. So I dug a little deeper only to find that you're nothing but a part-time ghost hunter. You're not even a doctor."

"Am I now?" said Tony. "Are you sure about that?"

Right on cue Johnathan's van came screeching into the car park.

"Come on Tony. We're late," he called through the open window.

The transit van was painted a medium blue with a green horizontal stripe running around it and two orange flowers. The words 'Mystery Machine' were emblazoned on its sides.

"He loves to make an entrance doesn't he?" said Janet.

"I hope there's no dog in there," said Tony, walking towards the van. "I hate dogs."

"Amateurs," muttered Simon.

Janet smiled as Tony clambered in alongside Johnathan. Tony looked back as the van left the car park to see the two police officers indulging in an animated discussion.

24

EVERYTHING LOOKED THE SAME, but it wasn't. Subtle changes were constantly confusing Tony, as though he were in the early stages of Alzheimer's. So many little things had changed, forcing him to pretend he had forgotten or make a wild guess.

Johnathan, for instance, was now much slimmer and athletic looking. The hearse had gone too, replaced by the Scooby Doo like Mystery Machine, which was equally embarrassing. Unsurprisingly, his head was starting to ache again.

Their conversation had been strained and awkward and now, after half an hour or so, Johnathan was clearly concerned at Tony's seemingly strange behaviour.

"What's my name, Doc?"

Tony paused. He'd assumed it would be the same but there was a possibility it was different, just like the security guard at the hospital. He decided to risk it.

"Johnathan," he said.

"Nope. It's Brian. And you should know that Doc."

"I'm sorry, yes of course it is. Brian. I was miles away there."

"Of course, it isn't. I'm Johnathan." He brought the van to a stop in a lay-by. "Look, what's going on mate? You've forgotten just about everything today."

"Sod it. Okay Johnathan I'll level with you, but I don't think you'll believe it."

Over the next twenty minutes Tony explained everything to Johnathan who, it turned out, was now his business partner. Having explained his remarkable tall tale, Tony waited for a reaction. He didn't wait long.

"Well why didn't you just tell me before?"

"You believe me?"

"Why wouldn't I? If you say it happened, it happened. If anyone else had trotted out that rubbish, I would have taken it with a pinch of salt but not you Tony."

Tony was relieved that Johnathan had taken it so well. It was also clear that he meant a lot to his young partner. He also now knew what he did instead of lecturing at the University. He was a partner in a ghost hunting business.

"So, what were we supposed to be doing at Longleat anyway?" he asked.

"Lord Bath hasn't been sleeping well," said Johnathan. "He thinks his house is haunted. We were going to check it out and see what was going on if anything. But from what you've just told me I think our time would be better spent hunting for this Pied Piper."

Tony thought the old Johnathan would have been a great asset in tracking him down, especially given all the equipment he used to have.

"Could you find a way of tracking him?"

"Maybe. As he's not of our time perhaps something will register. I don't know, is the honest answer."

"Do you still have plenty of testing equipment?"

"Filled to the bulkheads," said Johnathan, jerking his thumb behind him.

Tony peered through the small glass window into the rear of the van. There were stacks of silver flight cases, some free standing, some strapped to the walls, along with various other pieces of electronic equipment.

"Let's get back to King's Stanley and find this maniac before he hurts anyone else," said Tony.

"I'll tell the nitwit in knitting that we'll be there in a couple of days."

"Nitwit in knitwear?"

"Lord Bath. All his clothes are knitted."

"Everything?"

"Yeah, even his undercrackers. Anyway, he won't like it but, hey, who's he gonna call?"

Tony so wanted to say "Ghostbusters" but resisted in case the new Johnathan was as excitable as the old one. Besides the film might not have been made in this timeline. Was the Mystery Machine an improvement on the old hearse? He couldn't decide.

But it was good to know that this Johnathan was as eccentric as the other one. Tony smiled to himself.

25

"CAN WE STOP FOR a bit?" asked Tanya. "I'm tired and you must be too, carrying our baby."

"Okay but not for long," said Luuk. "I'm not sure how far Wicca magic can reach so I don't know if we're safe yet."

"Why are we walking Daddy?"

"We have no choice, little one. There are no cars or buses here in the Forest. When we reach Lymington we can catch a bus to the coast but until then we must walk."

Luuk eased Keterlyn to the floor. The little girl seized his hand, then her mother's.

"Don't let go," she said with a smile.

In an instant the three found themselves looking at a signpost. "Welcome to Lymington," it read.

"How did you do that?" asked Luuk. "Only ancient witches can travel that way."

Keterlyn beamed proudly.

"Remember she is the blessed one that Bathsheba chose to gift her powers to." Tanya bent down to hug her daughter.

"But she shouldn't reach her full magic potential for years yet, not until puberty at least."

"Maybe she hasn't. Perhaps she is just using a fraction of her powers until she matures."

"I'm tired," said Keterlyn. "Can we rest now that we are safe?"

Luuk looked around and spotted a barn in the distance. It looked old and unattended.

"We'll stay there for the night," he said, pointing.

The three weary travellers crossed a field of tall grass to reach their destination. Luuk tugged at the ancient door, opening it just wide enough to allow them inside. It was dark and damp, full of weeds and rotting hay. Rats could be heard scuttling out of the way of the intruders.

Tanya opened the palm of her hand and revived the floor in an instant with a pulse of energy, revealing it to be clean bare stone. With a wave of her hand bales of hay appeared from nowhere.

Meanwhile Luuk drew shapes in the air. A stone fireplace appeared, complete with lit fire and a pot bubbling with an appetising-smelling stew.

Keterlyn almost fell onto the nearest of the hay bales and fell instantly asleep. Her parents sat on bales close to the fire, warming their hands.

"If she hasn't reached her full potential yet she could end up having world ending powers," said Luuk. "She must learn the difference between good and bad magic. We need to teach her how to control the power she has and to learn to use it properly."

"Stop worrying Luuk. Don't forget she is our flesh and blood."

"And a lot of Bethsheba too."

Tanya cast a worried look at the sleeping child.

"You mustn't fear. We will take the time to teach her," said Luuk. "Now, do you want some of my famous nothing stew?"

"Why is it called nothing stew? Because it comes from nothing?"

"No. Once you try some you'll keep eating until there's nothing left," said Luuk with a chuckle.

"Oh very good. I'll be the judge of that. Now, aren't you forgetting something?"

Luuk pointed at the floor and three bowls and spoons appeared at their feet.

"Thank you," said Tanya and they both laughed.

The next morning Keterlyn woke first to see her parents still asleep in each other's arms. She also saw a bowl of stew sat on the floor by the still-burning fire and realised how hungry she was. Tucking in with relish, she found it tasted wonderful, like nothing she had ever eaten before. She soon finished and the noise of her spoon clattering into the empty bowl woke her mother.

She nudged her husband awake and the three of them sat around the fire.

"Are you feeling rested little one?" said Luuk. "You have a lot to learn today."

Keterlyn nodded.

"And have you had enough to eat?" asked her mother.

She nodded again.

"Coffee everyone?" said Luuk and in an instant steaming mugs were in each of their hands.

"Okay, first lesson," continued Luuk. "Never get lost. Always have an anchor to ground you. That's someone or somewhere that you can always return to in times of danger. Here and now, for instance."

Keterlyn closed her eyes, as did her mother.

"Try and remember the taste of the stew, the smell of the fire and the softness of the hay you slept on. All of this will make the memory clearer in your mind. Do you understand?"

Luuk took a sip of his coffee before continuing.

"If you need to be with us then all you have to do is remember the feel of when we hugged or the smell of your mother's perfume. But you must not try to be with someone who has passed over. Dreadful things happen if you try to interfere with the dead."

Keterlyn opened her eyes with a serious look on her face.

"You must never interfere with the dead. Ever. Do you understand me?"

"No, I won't," she said solemnly.

"Good magic will extend your life but bad magic will shorten it," continued Luuk, draining the last of his coffee. "Good magic is when you use it to help someone, you feed them or heal their wounds, not for your own benefit."

Tanya turned to her daughter to face her.

"Bad magic will age you faster than life itself," she said. "Bad magic is when you use your powers to hurt someone or, God forbid, kill them. Never, ever kill anyone. You will lose half your life force instantly."

"There are always other options," said Luuk. "You could disarm them or freeze them so they can't move. Make them sleep or forget something. No matter how bad they are you must never think about killing them. Do you understand little one?"

"Yes Daddy. I'm a good witch."

"Yes you are. One day you may be the most powerful witch in history so you must be careful not to show too many people your powers. There are bad people out there who will mean to do you harm."

"Do you mean other witches like us?"

"Yes, I'm afraid so. There are bad witches who want all the magic for themselves. Because they are bad they have to keep stealing magic to survive and that means stealing magic from you, me and your mother. We must all be very careful."

"I will be careful Daddy."

"If you feel threatened you must go to your happy, safe place, where they cannot find you," said her mother.

"Your last lesson for today," said Luuk, "is that you must never interfere with time itself. Do not try to change things in the past. We know you were lost back there and that couldn't be helped. You were attracted by the old magic of that rat catcher, a very evil man."

"Rattenfanger," said Keterlyn. Her face darkened and there was a slight growl in her voice.

"That's right," said her father. "So, what have we learnt today?"

"Don't get lost, be a good witch and I can't remember."

"Don't change the past," said Luuk, enveloping her in a huge hug.

"Can I change the future?"

Luuk and Tanya both smiled. For them it was a simple answer but for a six-year old, even one with the potential to be the most powerful witch that ever lived, it was a little harder.

"Yes baby you can change the future," said her mother. "You can change the future, because if you visit the past it would have to be changed again, unless you go back to that same time in the future again."

"So when is my past?"

"That's a very good question, little one," said Luuk. "You should be with us here and now in the year 1940. It is a time of great wars and great evil. When we finally found you in the future it was difficult for us to help you. Our powers are not as strong as yours. If you should end up in the future again we may not be able to help you."

"I think it is time for you to meet your great grandfather," said Tanya. "If anything should happen to us he will be the only one left who can help you."

Luuk wore a puzzled look. "But how?" he said.

"He will have to come to us. He is a long, long way in the past, even before you were in your cave Keterlyn. He is the greatest and most powerful wizard ever in the history of magic."

"But how will he know to come to us?" said Keterlyn.

"He will know and he will be here soon."

26

FRANKE HAD MADE A habit of checking every half hour or so to see if Keterlyn had returned to Room 212. This current visit was the fifth of the morning and she found the door ajar. Excitedly expecting to see the little girl in bed with her crayons, Franke pushed the door open. Instead, she found a large man, six foot or so, dressed in a black suit.

"This part of the hospital is off limits to the public sir," she said.

Fitch turned to face her.

"And so it should be. We wouldn't want them to find out about the little girl now, would we? Where is she now?"

Franke thought quickly. How did he know about Keterlyn? Was he another timeline blip?

"Who are you?" she said.

"Let's just say I'm an interested party, interested in all the goings on in this hospital."

Franke closed the door behind her and pressed the panic button by the light switch. Within moments footsteps could be heard running towards the room.

"Let's just say you're leaving immediately," said Franke, opening the door to reveal a hefty security guard. It was Roger. Or Steven. Whoever. What mattered was he was big and intimidating.

"Now hold your horses lovely," said Fitch, producing an identity card from inside his jacket. "National Security." He flashed it at her, too swiftly to be read, and replaced it in his jacket.

"You're way out of your jurisdiction and need to leave. Steven isn't it?" she said, turning to the guard.

"Yes Ma'am."

"Escort our friend here from the premises and make sure he doesn't enter again, unless he is seeking medical attention."

"Now wait a minute miss…"

"No, let's not wait. Thank you, Steven."

Steven took a step towards Fitch who immediately held up his hands, palms outwards. The guard began to frisk him and soon produced Fitch's gun from its shoulder holster. With a shocked look, Steven held it up for Franke to see before securing it in his belt behind his back.

"You brought a gun into a hospital?" said Franke. "What is the matter with you? Call the police Steven and let them deal with him. Be careful."

Steven placed a hand on Fitch's shoulder.

"Okay, okay. I'm going."

Steven manoeuvred him through the door and into the corridor where they were joined by a second guard. Franke watched them disappear down the corridor before once more peering into the room to make sure it really was empty. How had that man known about Keterlyn, she wondered, and who was he working for? It seemed bad news really did travel fast.

She realised that she should let Janet know what had happened. Maybe she could ensure he didn't return. Heading back to her office, she left a cryptic message for Janet on her answerphone.

Moving to the window, Franke was in time to witness the arrival of the Police Armed Response Unit. What sort of an imbecile brings a gun into a hospital, she wondered, relieved that nobody had been hurt. She had never seen a gun close up before. She had been angry at the time, now she was a little scared.

He's their problem now, she thought as she watched the police escort the handcuffed man dressed in black out to the van. He was bundled into the back and the van sped off.

She was startled by a knock at the door.

"Come in."

Steven entered.

"Thought I should check you're okay Miss Freud," he said, his soft voice a distinct contrast to his hulking frame.

"Thank you, Steven. That's sweet of you. I'm fine but what about you? I bet you don't have to take a gun off people too often."

"That was my first, to be honest. But as soon as I saw the gun my CP training kicked in."

"CP training?"

"Oh, close protection. I've worked as a bodyguard and part of the training was handling live firearms."

"Lucky for me."

"Lucky for us both. It was fully loaded and the safety wasn't engaged."

He suddenly seemed embarrassed and looked at the floor, rather than at her.

"Anyway, as long as you're alright miss, I'll get back to work." He turned to leave.

"Please call me Franke."

"Franke," he said, looking back. "Okay, see you later."

"Thanks again Steven," she said as he left.

"My pleasure," he said, closing the door.

27

ALL WAS QUIET WHEN Tony and Johnathan pulled into the King's Head car park. Tony noted that Janet's car was where they'd last seen it, but the ginger idiot's car was gone. So where was Janet? Silly question, he thought. In the pub having a coffee. She clearly couldn't go home while that guy was still living there.

"I'll check if Janet is in the pub," he said, getting out of the van.

He found her easily enough, sat at the bar with a large glass of something. Tony realised that the changes to the timeline had really taken a toll on her. The results were probably the worst she could have envisaged.

"Janet," he said as he walked up to her.

She immediately embraced him.

"What's wrong?" he asked.

"Nothing that a bullet in that ginger dick's face couldn't sort out. I'm glad you're here. I'm about to get very drunk."

She turned back to the bar.

"Another one of these and the same for my friend please barmaid. We're getting very drunk today."

"Oh no we're not," said Tony, stopping the barmaid with a wave of his hand. "We may have a way of tracking our friend."

"So what? It's not my case anymore." She drained her drink. "I resigned."

Tony took her shoulders and turned her to face him.

"Then all the more reason to help track down this maniac and stop him before he strikes again."

Tony kissed her before she could say anything more. When they broke off Janet spoke.

"Well, if you put it like that, lead the way."

In the car park Tony held the van door open for her to get in. They both joined Johnathan in the cab. After a moment Johnathan spoke.

"Aren't you going to introduce us?"

"What? You haven't met?" said Tony. "This is former Detective Sergeant Janet Walsh. Janet, this is my partner Johnathan, er, something."

Janet reached across and offered Johnathan her hand. To her surprise, he shook it rather than pressing his lips to it. This one was obviously not as gallant as the old one.

"Where to now?" asked Johnathan.

Tony looked at Janet.

"Start at Middleyard?" he said.

"Yes, that's the last place we saw him," said Janet.

"Great," said Johnathan. "Which way is that then?"

"Sorry," said Janet. "Turn right out of the car park and I'll tell you when to turn off." She snuggled back into the seat and pressed up against Tony.

"How much have you had to drink?" he said quietly.

"Enough," she said, smiling and snuggling some more.

A couple of minutes later Johnathan pulled the Mystery Machine to a halt on a gravelled parking area.

"Don't want to risk going down there," he said, pointing ahead to a narrow lane. "Only just got the sides lacquered and I don't want them scratched."

The three got out of the van and Johnathan slid open the side door to reveal the flight cases and assorted equipment.

"Okay, you get the EMF reader Janet."

He handed her a silver flight case with EMF printed on it.

"What exactly is an EMF reader?" she said.

"It's a must have for all ghost hunters," he replied. "All ghosts have an invisible electric energy around them, an electro-magnetic field, hence EMF. This reader detects that energy."

"Oh yes, of course. Silly me."

"The Air Ion Counter is for you Tony," said Johnathan, handing over what looked like a ray gun from a 60s comic.

"A what now?"

"It measures the positive and negative ions in the area. Ghosts give off an electromagnetic discharge so there should be a high positive ion count. Come on Doc, you know all this."

"But how is this going to help?" said Tony. "The Piper isn't a ghost."

"I've never had to search for a time traveller before, but it stands to reason that he's going to be giving off some kind of reading. Until we know what, we'll have to take everything."

"What are you taking?" asked Janet.

"I get the tranquiliser dart gun," he said, retrieving a rifle with a telescopic sight from the van. "Like you say, he's not a ghost and this might help."

He raised the rifle to check the scope, then pulled some clips of darts from a small case labelled 'Sleepy Time' and attached them to his belt. Finally, he picked out a sad old pith helmet and put it on.

"Lead the way," he said.

Janet laughed. "Johnathan the Big Game hunter," she said as they set off.

28

AN HOUR HAD PASSED and they had seen nothing and no-one. Having scanned Selsley Common and the various outbuildings in Middleyard and Penn Wood, their equipment hadn't found anything. After a further couple of hours, boredom had got to Johnathan and he had taken to shooting at random squirrels, magpies and passing cars, accompanied by the sounds of various machine guns and mortars.

Tony found himself dropping behind the others as he felt his age and the effects of his recent exertions. Meanwhile Janet's lunchtime drinks had worn off leaving her with the makings of a hangover. Tony appreciated that she was at least quiet.

Presently they came across two police constables, striding out with purpose. Johnathan hid his rifle as best he could and the others moved their flight cases out of obvious sight.

"What are you three doing along here?" One of them asked.

"Relax constable," said Janet. "I'm DS Walsh and these gentlemen are with me."

"Sorry Ma'am but we thought we were the last to go."

"What's happened? Has he been found?"

"No Ma'am but two children have gone missing from the common and everyone's been called in to search for them."

Janet turned to Tony, both of them visibly shocked.

"You two do what you've been told and we'll finish up here," she said to the policemen. Once they had gone, she turned to Tony again.

"You don't think he's up to his old tricks again so soon, do you?"

"I hope not but two kids going missing in his vicinity is a bit of a coincidence, isn't it?" he replied.

"We'd better head back," said Johnathan. "It'll be dark by the time we reach the van."

"I think you're right," said Tony. We'd best get off …"

"What did you say?" said Janet.

"Shut up," he snapped.

"Well, that's not very nice."

"Shut up and get down," he said, crouching down and pulling her arm.

"What's up Doc?" said Johnathan.

"Would you both be quiet," said Tony. "Look," he said, pointing at some nearby trees. "That's him. It must be."

"Those must be the missing children with him," said Janet. "Is it too far away to dart him from here Johnathan?"

"God yes. Even an expert shot, such as I, would need to be much nearer to have a chance of hitting him."

"Could you get a better shot from that hedge line?" said Tony, pointing.

"Maybe, if he keeps going in the same direction," said Johnathan, already creeping towards the hedge.

Tony and Janet stayed where they were, not wishing to risk spooking their quarry by making sudden movements. Tony saw Johnathan get into position, raise the rifle and adjust the sight. The Piper and the children were still heading in the same direction.

After a seeming eternity, a single shot rang out. Tony jumped up to look where the Piper had been but he was gone. He raised his shoulders and outstretched hands in Johnathan's direction and his partner raised a thumb in response.

Tony and Janet ran to join their companion.

"Did you get him?" she asked.

"Sure did."

"So where the hell is he?" said Tony.

"A wounded animal runs for cover," said Johnathan. "But in my experience, a single kiss from Jasmin here and he won't get far." He gave his rifle an affectionate pat.

"You call your gun Jasmin?" Said Tony, setting off towards the trees.

Johnathan was right and it only took them a few minutes to find the Piper slumped unconscious just inside the line of trees, flute in hand.

"We didn't think this through," said Tony.

"What do you mean?" said Janet.

"How are we going to get him back to the van?"

"And where are the kids." Janet frantically looked about her.

"Over there," said Johnathan. "Behind those trees."

Janet took off the way he was pointing. Finding the children, she crouched down a few feet away to be at their eye level.

"Don't be afraid," she said. "We're not going to hurt you."

Two girls aged around seven emerged from behind the trees, looked at each other and walked towards Janet.

"They look more confused than scared, if you ask me," said Johnathan.

"You could be right," said Tony. "Maybe he used the flute. But not again."

Tony prised the Piper's fingers apart and took the flute, pushing it into his pocket. It was too long to go in fully so a piece poked out.

Janet approached holding hands with the girls.

"I'll get these two back to their parents if you want to get that scumbag locked up somewhere until we decide what to do with him."

"Okay Janet. See you later back at mine," said Tony.

"I hope you don't mind, Tony, but I've nowhere else to go."

"Like I said, see you back at mine."

Janet smiled, first at Tony, then at the girls.

"Come on you two. Let's get you home. I bet your parents have been wondering where you've been."

Tony and Johnathan watched Janet and the girls as they made their way, hand in hand, along the dirt track by the hedge, chatting away as they went.

"Right, grab a leg," said Tony. "Let's get this piece of crap back to the Mystery Machine before he wakes up."

Tony seized one of the Piper's ankles, picking up the two flight cases with his other hand. Johnathan swung the rifle over his head, leaving both his hands free to grapple with the Piper.

"He won't be waking up any time soon, Doc."

"Glad to hear it."

The Piper's head seemed to hit every stone on the way down. Whether it was by design or accident was impossible to say.

"Anyway, why have you got those darts?" asked Tony.

"They were for the rhinos at Longleat. I worked there for Lord Bath a few years back before I went full time as a ghost hunter."

"Rhinos? No wonder he went down so fast. I'm surprised it didn't kill him. How long will he be out for?"

"They put a rhino out for forty-five minutes or so. For a human I would guess six to twelve hours."

They had come to a temporary halt and let the Piper fall to the ground.

"We mustn't forget that he hasn't done anything wrong in this timeline yet," said Tony.

"You call kidnapping two young girls with the probable intent of hanging them from a tree until they were dead nothing?"

"Well we don't know that was his intent this time."

"Okay, let's see," said Johnathan, beginning to search through their captive's pockets. He soon found a small knife and some lengths of rope. "Oh look. Tools of the trade."

Tony kicked the Piper square in the ribs.

"Let's turn this bastard face down and let his face eat some gravel on the way down," he said.

"Now you're talking. Shall we run?"

The two exchanged grins and, taking an ankle each, they set off along the gravel driveway down to the Mystery Machine.

Once there, Johnathan threw open the side doors and made a space amongst the flight cases.

"Let's tie him up and get him inside before anyone spots us," he said.

Using his own rope, they tied his hands and feet and managed to manoeuvre him into the van. His bloodied and scarred face looked up at them.

"That's got to hurt," said Tony, plucking a couple of pieces of gravel from their bloody pits in the Piper's face.

Johnathan tried to shut the door but only succeeded in slamming it into the Piper's head. They moved him further into the van and Johnathan shut the doors on his second attempt. The pair dragged themselves into the cab and paused to catch their breath.

"Now what are we going to do with him?" said Tony.

"I've got just the place," said Johnathan, starting up the van.

29

THEY WERE RIGHT AND it didn't take long before the great grandfather wizard appeared in the barn. He made his customary stealthy approach, ensuring he was never seen before he chose to be. Stepping from the shadows he made an impressive sight in a long, colourful cloak complete with cloth cap and a staff topped with a gem.

"Children," he said.

Three startled faces turned to see the grandfather of magic standing with open arms. Luuk and Tanya moved to embrace him while Keterlyn remained apart, watching.

"And who is this little one I see?"

Luuk moved aside.

"This is our daughter Keterlyn," he said.

The old man ran fingers through his beard.

"I sense great magic in you, Keterlyn."

"Thank you sir," she said somewhat nervously.

"Don't be afraid," he said. "Come here and let me get a good look at you."

Keterlyn moved towards the old man. When she was close enough she reached out and gave his beard a little tug.

"You look like my Daddy."

The old man laughed heartily.

"And you look just like your mother. Not forgetting that cheeky grin your father had when he was your age."

He knelt down to give her a hug.

"I can feel my old friend Bethsheba within you as well. I think you and I will become great friends."

"Thank you for coming grandfather," said Tanya. "We wanted Keterlyn to meet you in case anything should happen."

"I'm afraid a lot has happened already, my dear. I can sense a shift in future events as a result of magic in the past. The magic here is strong and it was easy to find you. And of course if I can find you easily, so can he. Judas."

"God, is he still alive?" said Luuk. "After his last massacre I thought he'd just fade away to nothing."

"Unfortunately not. His magic is now so strong that I fear I could do nothing to stop him should we meet."

Tanya embraced Keterlyn.

"What are we going to do?" she said.

"We must put Keterlyn in a time with no magic to allow her powers to grow. Allow Mother Earth to nourish her until she has reached her full potential. Only then do I feel she will be safe. But we must act quickly. Judas will be able to find us now we are all together in one place."

"Where will you take her?" asked Tanya, clinging tightly to her daughter.

"To a time in the future where she has already made a lasting impression and is missed. A safe place for her."

Luuk crouched down to join Tanya in embracing Keterlyn.

"It seems we aren't destined to all be together after all, little one," he said.

"We will always be around if you need us, your father and I and great grandfather," said Tanya. Looking at the wizard she added, "But she is so young. Is there really no other way?"

The old man studied them all for a moment.

"We must protect the good magic," he said. "There is too much evil in the world. Keterlyn may be the only one who can provide a balance between the old ways and she must be protected."

He struck his staff on the stone floor and the jewel produced a swirling vortex from floor to ceiling. He held out an arm.

"Come little one. Let's get you somewhere safe."

Keterlyn clung to her mother.

"It's okay, baby," said Tanya. "We'll all be watching over you and you'll see us again soon."

She gently ushered the girl towards the old man. Keterlyn took his hand and turned towards her father.

"Be strong, little one," he said.

"She will be safe and so must you be," said the great wizard. "Go now."

So saying he and Keterlyn stepped into the vortex and were gone.

30

THE SCOUT HUT WAS surrounded by police, cars and vans parked haphazardly, disregarding the allocated spaces. A buzz went round the crowd when they spotted Janet calmly approaching, hand in hand with the two missing girls. Cheers and applause greeted her as she brought the children to the doors of the hut.

One of them instantly broke away when she spotted her mother, the other was coaxed inside by Janet. DI Simon Bush was clearly upset.

"Thank you, DS Walsh," he said, trying to block her way. "That will be all."

"Trying to steal the credit again, Simon," she whispered, as she eased her way past him. "Hello everyone. I'm Detective Sergeant Janet Walsh and I was lucky enough to find the two girls in the woods up past the common."

A woman strode across the hall and wrapped Janet up in a huge hug.

"Thank you so much for bringing my baby home."

"All part of the service madam," said Janet, wiping away a tear.

"It was a team effort though," said Simon.

"Not really," Janet said. "After all, you're still here trying to get things organised, aren't you sir?"

Embarrassed, Simon moved outside and could be heard barking orders at anyone unfortunate enough to be able to hear him. Car doors could soon be heard slamming and engines being started as the car park began to empty.

Back in the hall Janet was happily soaking up praise and admiration from the parents and assorted friends, family and search volunteers. Simon returned.

"We are so glad to have been able to bring about such a speedy and positive outcome in this instance," he said.

He was blatantly trying to muscle in on the attention. That was his way. He knew he wasn't a great detective so had surrounded himself with those who were, like Janet. Then he was in the perfect position to take any praise for his subordinates' actions. It wasn't working today, however.

Simon was completely ignored as people gathered around to hear Janet's first-hand account of finding and returning the little girls. She in turn happily recounted her adventures, conveniently omitting mention of the Piper. Tony and Johnathan received name checks and ample praise, though. Mention of these two was more than her boss could stand and he raised his voice above the general hubbub so he could address Janet.

"Thank you, DS Walsh but you really should recommence your sick leave. Well done today but you should be resting at home."

It did not have the effect he desired as the crowd were now offering sympathy and praising her for rising from her sickbed to help. There was no possibility of Janet getting away home any time soon.

The ginger idiot had no option but to head outside once more, kicking over a waste bin in frustration as he did so.

31

JOHNATHAN WAS A VERY confident driver. He managed to break all the speed limits and take the many single track turns much too fast for Tony's liking. Which is why he hung onto the dashboard for the entire journey.

"No need to be nervous," said Johnathan. "My parents made me take rally cross lessons when I was fifteen. I'd taken my Police Advanced Driving Course by the time I was seventeen. I'm a good driver."

A sheep wandered into the road, forcing another controlled swerve.

"Well, most of the time," he added with a chuckle.

They came to an apparent dead end, a gate leading to a driveway running up to what appeared to be a stately home.

"What are you doing?" said Tony. "This is clearly private property."

"No worries, Doc. I know the owner quite well."

Having manoeuvred the Mystery Machine up the driveway and around a large central fountain, Johnathan brought the van to a halt at the foot of a set of stone steps leading up to an imposing manor house.

"Wow," said Tony. "What a place."

"It was built in the Gothic Revival style in 1887, custom built and designed for Lord Stanton, believed to be a close friend of Queen Victoria herself."

"Lord Stanton? Never heard of him," said Tony, gazing up at the house admiringly.

"The family always kept themselves to themselves."

The three-storey mansion stood as it always had amongst sweeping lawns and a mass of mature trees. Hand crafted from sandstone, it featured Lancet stained-glass windows above the atrium and vaulted cathedral-like ceilings.

"Last estimate valued it at around four million," said Johnathan. "It's got twenty bedrooms, a ballroom and two kitchens. Not big ones, mind. Well, the one downstairs is but I tend to use the smaller one for snacks and stuff when I stay."

Johnathan clambered out of the van.

"There's lots of state rooms, even a boot room, but most importantly the cellar has a dungeon."

"Why would Lord Stanton need a dungeon?"

"It's where he kept his wine from his alcoholic wife and in modern times it's been converted to a soundproof panic room. Which makes it perfect for you know who."

Tony climbed down.

"I suppose I could slum it here for a bit," he said.

Johnathan slid open the side door to find the Piper still out for the count. Before they could remove him, a voice spoke from the front of the van.

"Ah, Master Stanton. Nice to see you again. Will you be staying?"

Tony's eyes were drawn to a tall man, formally dressed in a black suit, white shirt and black tie.

"This is Parker, the family butler," said Johnathan. "Yes, for a while Parker, and I'm expecting friends. Make up a couple of the guest bedrooms would you? And we have a guest for the basement too so we'll need to clear the junk out of the cells."

"Of course sir," said the butler. "I'll unlock the basement doors." He headed back up the stone steps.

"So this is your house?" said Tony, mouth agape.

"I'm not one to brag buddy."

"And you're a Lord too?" They began dragging the Piper from the van. "Well don't think I'm going to call you sir."

"Yes, that's me. Lord John Thomas Stanton the Fifth. Or Penis Boy as I was called at Eton. Thankfully I can't pass the title down to my children, when I have any. The Government changed the rulings in 1999 so they can make their friends, party donors and MPs Lords and Ladies when they retire or become too unpopular to remain in the Commons."

"Penis Boy? Eton? Lord Do-dah the Fifth? How did I not know all this?"

"Like I said, I'm not one to brag. Come on Doc. Let's get this piece of trash round the side before he wakes up."

Grabbing an arm each, they dragged the Piper round to the left side of the mansion. There they found Parker waiting for them, standing by the coal chute whose two heavy doors had been propped open.

"Do you want me to carry him or drop him down the chute sir?" asked Parker.

"We'll carry him," said Tony. "He's suffered enough today."

They struggled to get the Piper to his feet, slung an arm over each of their shoulders and carried him down the concrete steps into the basement.

"Drop him here for a bit and help me clear the cage out," said Johnathan as their eyes slowly acclimatised to the gloom of the cellar.

Hanging up his jacket and rolling up his shirtsleeves, Parker mucked in with them. They had soon moved the various old chairs, paintings and dust-laden cases of wine, leaving the cage completely empty.

"Shall I run the Edward through before putting him in sir?" asked Parker.

"Don't bother," said Johnathan. "He's used to dirt and muck. Let's just get him in and lock the door so we can all take a breath."

They dragged the Piper into the cage and Parker closed and locked its old iron door. Handing the key to Johnathan, the retainer led the two of them up the staircase and into the main building.

The basement stairs led into the atrium with the towering Lancet stained-glass window. Parker ushered them through into a reception room equipped with a snooker table, dartboard and large well-stocked bar. Johnathan immediately positioned himself behind the bar.

"Can I get you something Tony?" he asked.

"Can I have a Pepsi?"

"What the hell kind of cocktail is that?"

"It's a soft drink," said Tony. "Pepsi Cola. You must know it."

"Still not drinking then. Good for you." Johnathan rummaged through the various bottles and checked the fridge. "No Pepsi I'm afraid. Will Coke do?"

"Yes that's fine. I can't believe you've never heard of Pepsi though."

"I'll have Parker order some for your next visit," said Johnathan, handing over a cold can.

"Are you okay if I tell Janet to meet us here?" said Tony. "She was supposed to staying at mine."

"Mi casa su casa, buddy," said Johnathan taking a swig of brandy from a crystal goblet. "I've asked Parker to make up a couple of rooms for you both. Cheers."

32

JANET WAS PLEASED TO hear from Tony again. Having called round at his place and found it empty she had naturally been worried. He and Johnathan were alone with the Piper after all.

What a thought that was. The real-life Pied Piper of Hamelin was alive and well after eight hundred years. She was well aware of his heinous crimes, of course, although he had done little in this age. Back in the day legend had it he played his pipe and danced away with one hundred and thirty of the children of Hamelin, never to be seen again.

At least not until now, eight hundred years later, when a young witch called Keterlyn became entangled in his scheme and found herself hanging with them in the trees.

Janet recalled the scene in the woods perfectly. She saw the children of Hamelin, friends of Keterlyn, hanging from the trees and branches. What must it have been like for them? How scared they must have been. What had that sadistic maniac done to their tiny bodies before draping them there?

She shivered as she turned into the private driveway of Stanton Manor, trying to shake the images from her mind. They were banished immediately she saw the imposing building before her. She had imagined Johnathan's abode to be a cottage at best, but this!

Tony stood on the steps waving as she circled the fountain and brought the car to a halt.

"You made it then," he said as she exited the aging Granada. "Didn't get lost?"

"No, I think I *am* lost. Johnathan lives here? Rich parents then."

Janet pulled her suitcase from the boot and made her way up the steps as Tony came down them to meet her.

"I'm afraid it's all his. Come on," he said, taking her case in one hand and her hand in the other. "I'll give you the grand tour."

He showed her the large reception room converted to Johnathan's playroom and enjoyed the look of amazement on her face as they entered the ballroom with its stained-glass windows and chandeliers. They visited four or five luxurious bedrooms before walking into an especially impressive one with dual aspect.

"I took the liberty of nabbing this one for us," he said with a smile. "Of course, you can have one of your own if you'd prefer."

"This will do. I don't mind slumming it." She smiled back at him.

"That's exactly what I said to Johnathan when I first clapped eyes on the place."

"Say, where is Johnathan by the way?"

"Lord John Thomas Stanton the Fourth. Or was it Fifth? Whatever. He went down to the dungeon to check on the prisoner."

"Dungeon?" said Janet.

"Yes. Actually, he went down there some time ago. We'd best check he's okay."

Hand in hand they made their way through the opulent accommodation and down the small staircase leading to the basement rooms.

"You really meant a dungeon, didn't you?" said Janet as they descended into the darkness. "I thought you were joking."

As Tony's eyes adjusted to the blackness he realised something was wrong. The Piper was growling in his cage like a rabid animal, which was to be expected. But Johnathan and Parker were standing with their hands in the air. At first Tony thought the madman had them under a spell of some kind, but didn't he need the flute for that? "Johnathan," he called.

"Oh hi Doc," Johnathan replied. "We're in a spot of bother I'm afraid."

A figure stepped from the gloom, causing Janet to jump and grab Tony's arm.

"Who the hell are you?" said Tony.

The figure in black jabbed a gun at them.

"Nice of you to join us," he said. "I'm sorry we had to start without you." He waved the gun in the direction of Johnathan. "Now over there and keep your hands where I can see them."

"Says his name is Fitch," said Johnathan. "American Secret Service or something. You're well out of your jurisdiction here old boy. Oh hi Janet. This is Parker, my Butler."

"Pleasure to meet you madam," said Parker.

"Thank you. Not the most convenient of times," said Janet, holding out her hand.

"Indeed madam."

"Enough already!" barked Fitch. "Smallman. Pat them down."

Another figure emerged from the shadows and ran his hands over them, presumably checking for weapons.

"Watch where those hands go," said Janet. "Pervert."

Smallman slapped her face and Tony made a move towards him, only stopping when a second gun was produced and waved in his face. Having finished his work, Smallman nodded at Fitch and once more stepped back into the shadows.

"Now I want to know what's going on around here," said Fitch. "As far as I can see you are holding someone in a cage against their will. There are a lot of laws being broken around here. I want to know who he is and where the girl is."

The girl, thought Tony. Could he mean Keterlyn? How the hell did he know about her? What could he know about her? Did he now as much as they did or was he just fishing? Tony decided it was the latter.

"What girl?" he said.

"The girl from the thirteenth century. The time traveller."

"Was she about six years old with blonde hair?" said Tony.

"Tony!" yelled Janet in surprise.

"Yeah, that's her."

"Never seen her," said Tony with a smile, as the others laughed. They stopped when Fitch hit Tony across the head with the gun. Tony dropped to his knees.

"Wise guy, huh?" said Fitch. "There's one in every pack."

Janet took Tony's arm. He touched the back of his head and saw blood. He took a step towards Fitch who raised the gun.

"Tony, don't," said Janet.

"It's not worth it Doc," added Johnathan.

Tony was furious.

"Who do you think you are invading this house without authority? Think you're a tough guy standing there holding a gun. How about going a round with me here and now, eh?"

"Don't be foolish Tony," said Janet, still hanging onto his arm.

"You should listen to your bitch," said Fitch.

"Who are you calling a bitch?" snapped Janet, making to move on him.

Fitch pulled back the gun's hammer. The sound was enough to stop Janet in her tracks.

"Just tell me about the girl and this can all be over," said Fitch. "How did she get here and where is she now?"

"Screw you," said Tony. "We're not telling you anything."

"I had hoped this would have gone a little better," said Fitch. "Let's start again. My name is Agent Fitch and I work for the American Secret Service. Well, a subdivision of them anyways. My colleagues and I have been tasked with finding out about the girl from the hospital, how she can apparently appear and disappear at will, transporting people wherever and whenever she wants. Now, does that ring any bells?"

Tony and Janet looked at each other, amazed that he knew so much.

"I can see that it does," said Fitch. "So where is she?"

"The honest truth is that we don't know," said Janet. "Now will you just leave us alone?"

"If I were a betting man I'd say you were telling me the truth," said Fitch. "But it's nothing I don't already know."

Janet screamed at him.

"What do you want to know!"

Fitch screamed back.

"Where is the girl!"

Pointing the gun at the ceiling, he fired a single shot. Dust and small pieces of plaster settled at his feet.

"You'll pay for any damage," said Johnathan calmly.

"I'm sure you can afford it, Lord Snooty," said Fitch.

There was a sudden crash from the cage. The Piper had tried to smash his way out using the small stool in there with him.

"Maybe I should put the girl in there," said Fitch. "Who the hell is he anyway?"

"That's my cousin Hubert," said Johnathan. "He's a bit mentally unstable these days so we thought it's the best place for him."

"I see. Well come on, beautiful, in you go," said Fitch, taking Janet by the arm. "I'm sure Hubert will appreciate the company. Unless you've anything you'd like to share with me."

"You can't do that," said Tony.

Fitch pointed the gun in his direction and fired.

"Tony!" screamed Janet.

Tony was still standing and patted himself down. He felt no pain and could find no bullet hole. He looked at Fitch and found him mesmerised, staring at a single bullet spinning in the air between them but making no forward progress. Then it simply dropped to the floor with a ping.

Fitch looked at his gun, only to see it wrenched from his grasp by some invisible force. Smallman and a third man emerged from the shadows, floating a foot or so above the ground. They were clearly struggling against something that couldn't be seen.

Fitch felt himself seized under the arms and across his torso by a vice-like grip. He struggled against it but in vain and he soon found himself floating alongside his colleagues.

The three guns now hovered in front of them, tantalisingly out of reach. They began to glow, seemingly white hot, then folded and moulded into each other. With a hiss of steam, they were melded together and dropped to the floor with a clang.

33

OUT OF THE SHADOWS stepped Keterlyn. She was dressed as they found her amongst the trees wearing a simple white dress and going barefoot.

Tony felt a wealth of emotions flood over him, relief for his escape from near-death and joy at seeing Keterlyn again back amongst them. He reached out his arms.

"Keterlyn."

She ran to him, throwing herself into his arms. Tony was surprised but welcomed her nonetheless. Once again, she reminded him of his own lost daughter. Janet joined them and added to the embrace.

"Where have you been?" she said. "Are you alright?"

"I am fine, thank you very much," said Keterlyn.

"You can speak to us now?" said Tony.

"Yes, grandfather has taught me how." She pointed back to the shadows. "This is grandfather."

A figure emerged. He was clearly an old man with a long white beard. His whole frame was enveloped by a colourful cloak and on his head he wore a small cloth hat, similar to a beret. In his left hand he held a staff with a glowing gem atop. His right hand was held palm outward and it was clear he was controlling events here, not Keterlyn.

"It's a pleasure to meet you sir," said Tony, rising to his feet.

"The pleasure is all mine," said the old man. "And you have my gratitude, Tony and Janet, for taking care of the little one."

He spoke with a deep, gravelly voice that reverberated throughout the walls of the dungeon.

"You know our names?" said Janet.

"I see and hear everything I want to, from the past, present and future. This timeline has been damaged. It must be repaired before this alternative reality becomes a fixed point in time."

"Yes, sorry about that," said Tony. "It wasn't done on purpose. We didn't know the Pied Piper would tag along for the ride."

"Yes, he is a troublesome magical creature who needs to be returned to his own time," said the old man.

A voice came from above their heads.

"The Pied Piper?" said Fitch. "The Pied Piper of Hamelin? But how can he …"

But Fitch found he was unable to finish his sentence. In fact, no matter how hard he tried, he could utter no more words at all.

"What about them?" said Tony, jerking his thumb at the ceiling.

"They will not remember anything once I restore the timeline," said the old man. "Nobody will. All will be well again."

"Who are you?" asked Johnathan.

"I have been known by many names through the ages. Lately they seem to be calling me Merlin the Enchanter."

"Bloody hell," said Parker, surprising everyone with his crudity. "Merlin from the legends of King Arthur?"

"I am currently in the service of Uther Pendragon, but Arthur will soon be king and will unite the land within his rule."

"I don't understand," said Janet. "If you can travel between times, why choose to live, in an age so long ago?"

"I may be able to span time, but my place is neither in the future nor the past. I must be where I need to be. For now, that is in Camelot at the court of Uther Pendragon."

"Grandfather is the greatest wizard who will ever live," said Keterlyn, moving to stand beside him. "Isn't that right pop-pop?"

"I feel my power will pale compared to yours when you reach maturity, my little witch," said the old man, resting a hand on her head.

Janet clasped Tony's hand tightly.

"What's going to happen now?" he said.

"Everything will return to how it was and how it is meant to be," said Merlin. "You will not remember anything and no harm will have been done."

"But what if we want to remember?" said Janet. "We've only just met and there is no way our paths would cross normally."

"Yes, please let us remember," added Tony.

"Highly irregular," said Merlin then paused for a moment. "But there may be a way."

Keterlyn tugged at his sleeve and he bent down to let her whisper in his ear.

"If, you're sure?" he said and Keterlyn nodded her head. "Very well."

Merlin drew himself up to his full height and cleared his throat before continuing.

"Dr Small and Miss Walsh, would you be willing to take charge of Keterlyn and raise her as your own? Will you teach her the virtues of right and wrong and educate her in your ways? This is a most solemn undertaking, but I believe it is high time there was some good magic in this age."

Tony looked at Janet. They smiled simultaneously and nodded their heads.

"We'll do it, if she'll have us," said Tony.

Keterlyn ran to them and hugged them both.

"One condition," said Janet. "We keep our memories of what has happened. It will help us protect her in the future."

"Then it is settled," said Merlin.

He raised his glowing staff and a rush of wind filled the dungeon. Everything seemed drawn towards it and soon the room filled with dust and debris. A mini tornado was created.

Tony hung on desperately to Janet and Keterlyn. The three men in black hanging in mid-air could not avoid being drawn into the vortex and, one by one, they disappeared.

The Piper was hanging onto the bars of the open cage. His struggles were futile though and soon enough he was forced to let go. He too vanished into the spout of the tornado.

Johnathan leapt gleefully into the air.

"See you on the other side," he shouted as he vanished.

Parker merely smiled as he was engulfed by the magic wind from nowhere.

The wind died down and everything became dark and still until, at last, everything was quiet.

34

TONY, JANET AND KETERLYN climbed the concrete steps from the cellar, hand in hand, and stepped out into the daylight. Tony didn't know what day it was and felt unclear where Merlin had sent them timewise. He reasoned that Janet had arrived in the evening and, after an hour of sheer chaos, it was surely too early to be light.

He sat Keterlyn in a seat in the back of Janet's decaying Granada, ensuring her seat belt was fastened, then climbed into the back himself. This made Janet feel a bit like a chauffeur but she was pleased with the way he was caring for their new charge.

Tony caught her eye in the rear-view mirror and smiled.

"I suppose you'll be single again now everything is back to normal," he said.

"Thank god for that."

"No, thank pop-pop," said Keterlyn.

"Yes, thank pop-pop for getting everything back to normal," said Janet. "Providing it is all back to normal. You'll have your job back at the University, Tony."

"Hopefully," he replied. "I enjoy the place and Stephen is … Stephen, of course. Janet we need to make a pit stop. And can you turn the radio on. What time is it?"

"What day is it, more like," said Janet, switching on the radio.

After playing a couple of songs and some adverts the DJ announced it was ten o'clock on Wednesday 4th October.

"Perfect," said Tony. "Stephen is always in on a Wednesday and lectures second period. Keterlyn, I want you to meet a good friend of mine."

Janet turned the radio down and steered the car through the back lanes onto the main roads.

"Why do you want her to meet Stephen?" she asked as she drove up the slip road and onto the M5.

"If she still has her magic she may be able to help my oldest friend. He has been diagnosed with inoperable cancer." Turning to Keterlyn he said, "Do you still have magic?"

Keterlyn said nothing. She was gazing out of the window at the many cars on the busy motorway.

One caught her eye and she watched it as it sped past and eventually disappeared way ahead of them. She looked at Tony, then touched the side panel of the car with a single, tiny finger. Her face became a study in concentration.

Strange things started to happen to Janet. She felt her sitting position shape change and the steering wheel seemed to grow in her hands. In an instant the ageing Granada had become a brand-new Mustang.

Tony sank back into the plush leather seats and looked at Keterlyn. She smiled and in turn he caught Janet's eye in the now much larger rear-view mirror and smiled too. Janet accelerated to overtake the car in front, laughing as she did so.

"Thank you Keterlyn," she said.

The journey back to UWE featured much revving of the new car's engine as Janet enjoyed the deep throated roar it made. There were plenty of smiles and laughter, mainly from Janet as she experienced the joy the new Mustang gave her.

Eventually they turned into the staff car park at the University, the engine still growling.

"My space should be just there," said Tony, pointing to one between two parked cars marked with a white 26.

After Janet had parked they made their way into the main campus building and into the Lecture Theatre Reception area.

"You two wait here while I check that things are back to normal and I still have a job here."

Tony made his way into the Lecture Theatre, standing at the back of the hall. He saw his friend and, to Tony's relief, Stephen smiled at him.

"We will finish early so you may take this last twenty minutes as planning time," Stephen said to the students. "Work out what you want to say then think about the details. How you will structure your argument and what needs to be included to support it. I will see you all again on Friday morning when we will start your final dissertations. Dismissed."

Some thirty students stood noisily, gathering their bags and books and heading out of the hall.

Tony spotted a student he recognised.

"Hello sir."

"Hello Russell," Tony replied, before making his way down the steps towards his friend.

Tony held out his hand which Stephen grasped enthusiastically.

"Tony," said the Chancellor. "To what do I owe this unexpected pleasure?"

Tony noticed that he looked especially pale and drawn today.

"I wondered if you had time to discuss something important," he said.

"Of course. Everything alright?"

"Yes. I want you to meet someone."

As they began to climb back up the stairs of the hall, Stephen spotted a departing student.

"Riley, your punishment ends tomorrow not today. Whiteboards thank you."

The student reluctantly headed back down the stairs.

Tony opened the door and held it for his friend. They found Janet and Keterlyn waiting for them.

"Let's go to my office for some privacy," said Stephen, leading them to a large wooden door by the main entrance bearing the words 'Prof S Williams. Chancellor', in proud gleaming gold letters.

When they were all inside and seated with the door shut, Tony began the introductions.

"Professor Williams this is Detective Inspector Janet Walsh. She called at the University last week, you may recall."

"Ah yes. The problem in the field." Stephen held out his hand. "Hope that's all been sorted out satisfactorily?"

"Yes it has been," said Janet, shaking his hand. "Thanks to Tony."

Stephen crouched down to Keterlyn's eye level.

"And who have we got here?"

"I'm Keterlyn. How do you do sir?" She held out her hand.

"Well aren't you the sweetest thing ever." Stephen shook her hand and turned to Janet. "Is she yours?"

"Well, er" began Tony. "It's a long story Stephen. Suffice to say we are looking after Keterlyn for a while."

"Spill the beans old man. I've finished for the day and have all the time in the world."

Tony cast a questioning look at Janet who replied with a shrug of her shoulders and a brief nod. So for the next half hour they regaled Stephen with an account of their adventures, trying not to talk over each other in their enthusiasm to tell the tale accurately. Keterlyn, meanwhile, amused herself by wandering around the Chancellor's office, picking up random books or artefacts that he had collected on his travels over the years as a student and educator.

They were interrupted by a knock at the door. A woman entered carrying a tray with tea and biscuits and a single glass of cloudy lemonade, complete with a straw. She slid the tray onto the desk before taking her leave.

"Thank you Beryl," said the Chancellor. "Shall I be mum?" he added, pouring the tea. "I must admit you tell a fascinating story, but you can't expect me to believe it without any corroborating evidence." He held out the glass. "Keterlyn?"

"Its Keterlyn," said Janet. "Say thank you Keterlyn."

The girl gingerly took the glass and looked at Tony. "Go on. It's okay," he said.

"Thank you sir," she said, taking a sip from the side of the glass and nearly poking herself in the eye with the straw. She pulled a face.

"I can get you another flavour if you like," said Stephen.

"I like strawberries," she said, dipping her finger into the glass. The liquid turned bright red.

Stephen stared.

"That sort of evidence?" said Tony.

"How did you do that?" asked Stephen.

Keterlyn thought for a moment, looking at Tony then Janet before replying.

"I'm a witch."

35

THEY SPENT A FURTHER twenty minutes explaining the finer points of their story to the Chancellor who asked various questions which required explanation, elaboration and, finally, trust.

"But if I do believe you, why are you here? Why are you telling me this tale?"

Keterlyn placed her empty glass on the desk and leant in close to him, whispering in his ear.

"You need help sir," she said.

"And how can you help me?" he whispered back.

Keterlyn stepped back and clapped her hands. Again and again she clapped, each seeming louder and fiercer than the previous one.

Stephen looked afraid and tried to speak but found he could not. The next clap made him shudder and each one now seemed to make him twitch and move involuntarily.

Tony cast a puzzled look at Janet. He had asked Keterlyn to help kill the cancer that was eating his friend alive but he had expected something more restrained, such as a touch of a finger.

Keterlyn's clapping continued and now the very room seemed to shake. Books fell from shelves and the desk began to move away from the Chancellor who found himself backed into the corner of the room.

Stepping closer to him, Keterlyn's next clap lifted him bodily into the air before he slumped in a heap on the floor before her. Gathering himself he looked up at the small girl who offered him her hands to help him rise to his feet.

Assuming it was all over, Tony moved to help.

"Wait," said Keterlyn. "We must let the sickness out."

"What?" said Stephen. "How?"

"You must vomit."

"I can't I don't want to."

"You must," she said, launching herself at him and forcing her tiny hand into his mouth.

Tony could hear his friend choking and spluttering. Finally, Keterlyn removed her hand and Stephen spewed copiously. He convulsed, retching to empty the final contents of his stomach.

There on the floor between his feet was a mass of blood, skin and sinew.

"What the hell is that?" said Janet.

"The bad that was inside him," said Keterlyn. "There was a lot of it."

She stumbled a step towards Tony and made to fall. He was quick enough to catch her.

"I've got you," he said as she closed her eyes and fainted.

"Is she alright?" asked Janet.

"Yes, but it must have taken a lot out of her."

"Him too, by the look of that hairball," said Janet. She helped Stephen to a chair. "Are you okay?"

"I feel weird," he said. "Empty. And very hungry."

"We'll take that as a good sign," said Tony.

"What just happened to me?"

"Keterlyn is a witch and has great powers," said Tony. "But being so young and physically small it takes a lot out of her."

"But what did she do to me?"

"I think she removed the cancer from inside you," said Janet. "That's it on the floor there."

"That was inside me?" said the Chancellor and gave the mass a small kick. "That is the cancer?"

"We think so, so best not touch it," said Tony. "We should just get rid of it."

Stephen seemed unable to tear his eyes away from the mass on the floor.

"I think I will donate it to the Science Department, if that's alright with you," he said.

"Go for it," said Tony. "But you can't disclose where it came from. Ever."

"If you ask me, we should just drop it in the incinerator," said Janet.

Tony sank down into a chair cradling Keterlyn in his arms.

"You know, she has so much power, but is still vulnerable," he said.

"Maybe that's why Merlin wanted her cared for," said Janet, taking the chair next to him. "He didn't want her left on her own again."

"Stephen, you can't tell anyone about this," said Tony. "When the doctors find you in remission it must be seen as a miracle or something."

"Of course. And who would believe me anyway?"

They all laughed, releasing some of the tension in the room.

"If it is true and I am free of it then you'd best take very good care of that little one with the gift of the gods."

Janet and Tony looked at each other and down at the sleeping child.

"We will," they said in unison.